PENGUIN WORKSHOP
An Imprint of Penguin Random House LLC, New York

The publisher does not have any control over and does not assume any responsibility for author or third-party websites or their content.

This publication contains the opinions and ideas of its authors. It is intended to provide helpful and informative material on the subjects addressed in the publication. It is sold with the understanding that the authors and publisher are not engaged in rendering medical, health, or any other kind of personal professional services in the book. The reader should consult his or her medical, health, or other competent professional before adopting any of the suggestions in this book or drawing inferences from it.

The author and publisher specifically disclaim all responsibility for any liability, loss, or risk, personal or otherwise, which is incurred as a consequence, directly or indirectly, of the use and application of any of the contents of this book.

Photo credits: letter balloons: Symphonie Ltd/Culture/Getty Images

Text copyright © 2019 by Michael I. Bennett and Sarah Bennett.
llustrations copyright © 2019 by Penguin Random House LLC. All rights reserved.
Published by Penguin Workshop, an imprint of Penguin Random House LLC, New York.
PENGUIN and PENGUIN WORKSHOP are trademarks of Penguin Books Ltd, and the W colophon is a registered trademark of Penguin Random House LLC.
Printed in the USA.

Visit us online at www.penguinrandomhouse.com.

Library of Congress Cataloging-in-Publication Data is available upon request.

ISBN 9781524787905   10 9 8 7 6 5 4 3 2 1

LIFE SUCKS

How to Deal with the Way Life Is, Was, and Always Will Be Unfair

BY **MICHAEL I. BENNETT, MD** and **SARAH BENNETT**

ILLUSTRATED BY **BRIDGET GIBSON**

PENGUIN WORKSHOP

TABLE OF CONTENTS

Introductions Suck: Five Facts About This Book 1

How This Book Works 5

Chapter 1: Friendship Sucks 9

Chapter 2: School Sucks 45

Chapter 3: Cultural Differences Suck 79

Chapter 4: Bodies Suck 113

Chapter 5: Homes Suck 152

Chapter 6: Sexuality Sucks 184

Acknowledgments 223

Further Resources 229

To Mona, who accepted me forty-three years ago as a work in progress and continues to give me tolerance and love that I don't always deserve

—MB

To Mr. Dale DeLetis, my eighth-grade English teacher and high-school academic advisor. Without his encouragement, passion for literature, and utter refusal to suffer my sulky adolescent BS, I never would have survived middle or high school, aka the suckiest years of my life

—SB

INTRODUCTIONS SUCK:
FIVE FACTS ABOUT THIS BOOK

Whether we're a preschooler or a young teen, a graduating college senior or a retired person, we human beings all want to know that we're acceptable, that our being alive somehow makes a difference in the lives of others.

—Fred Rogers, *The World According to Mister Rogers: Important Things to Remember*

FACT #1: This book contains no magical answers or the keys to self-help, happiness, flawless contouring, etc.

Our experience has taught us that no matter what so many self-help books and well-intentioned therapists, teachers, and counselors tell us, those answers don't exist. And pushing yourself to find them instead of dealing with what you've got will make you more frustrated, miserable, and mad at yourself. So even if this book doesn't hold the secrets to fixing all your problems, it will show you how to develop your own unique problem-management skills.

FACT #2: This book makes one promise—that life is hard, but never impossible.

The only guarantee we can make is that life is difficult and often painful. And so many of the major factors that influence our lives, from the way other people act to our own emotional responses to things, are completely out of our control. Instead of learning to blindly trust and act on our feelings when it comes to making important decisions, it's better to look for guidance from facts, experience, and the pride that comes from achieving the least-crappy outcome in an altogether crappy, miserable situation. In other words, we've found that your heart is full of blood and your gut is literally full of crap, so it's best to follow your brain instead.

FACT #3: This book will ask you to give up on wild expectations, but not to give up on yourself and on doing the right thing.

Giving up on false hope doesn't mean giving up, period. It just means letting go of your unrealistic wishes for what you hoped would happen, figuring out what aspects of the problem you can control, and readjusting your goals accordingly. The only thing you're actually giving up is endlessly punishing yourself and feeling like a failure for no good reason.

FACT #4: Although this book's for not-yet-adults, it's really for everyone.

In theory, this book is aimed at not-yet-adults. We wanted to write a book especially for them, in plain English, about how to deal with life's biggest issues, if only to try to reach readers early enough in life to save them some misery in the future. In reality, however, solid advice isn't limited to any one age group. That's because many of the most painful problems in life—no matter your age—stem from feeling different and alone, and feeling like an isolated weirdo can make anyone see themselves as a failure.

FACT #5: Although this book will not necessarily make you feel better, it will make you better at dealing with life.

In fact, if this book does promise any keys to life's difficulties, it's one so simple and obvious that we have no problem sharing it before the book's even officially started. And that is: When the problem tormenting you is unsolvable, at least for the foreseeable future, the best way to get through it is to stay focused on doing your best to be a good person, despite how crappy you feel and how hard things are.

Our advice will give you methods for managing problems when happiness is not an option. It will also help you rate yourself, not on how much you've achieved, but on how hard you tried to do the right thing when good results and happiness just weren't possible. And at the end of the day, that's all any of us, at any age, can truly hope for. Even if most people or books won't admit it, especially in an introduction.

HOW THIS BOOK WORKS

STRUCTURE:

Each chapter of this book will cover a big thing in your life that can suck: friendship, school, cultural differences, bodies, homes, and sexuality. Feeling like you don't measure up to others in these areas—like you have too few friends or look too different—can make you feel more isolated, miserable, and generally sucky than any one person should have to put up with.

Then, instead of telling you how to feel better, or offering solutions you've already thought of, we challenge you to use your own experience and sense of right and wrong to fight all the undeserved and unfair negative feelings and find a way forward. That's why each chapter begins with a simple quiz to help you determine what your own values are and whether you're living up to them—despite what you hear from parents, teachers, guidance counselors, and others or from your own negative feelings—or whether there's room to improve and change.

The chapters are then broken down into sections. Each one will use examples to illustrate advice for specific problems, separating realistic goals from false hopes. We'll also help you decide what feedback is worth paying attention to and what's negative and unimportant, even if it's coming from those who mean well and really want to help. We'll then offer realistic suggestions, not to fix or solve, but to manage those issues and the powerful, crappy feelings they cause. The advice will be broken down along these lines:

- **SIGNS YOU MAY BE MISINTERPRETING THINGS**
- **. . . AND SIGNS YOU AREN'T**
- **WHAT YOUR PARENTS SAY TO TRY TO HELP**
- **. . . AND WHY IT ISN'T HELPFUL AT ALL**
- **WHAT YOU THINK YOU NEED TO FIGURE OUT IN ORDER TO FIX IT**
- **WHY THOSE FIXES WILL FAIL**
- **WHAT YOU CAN ACTUALLY DO ABOUT IT**
- **RED FLAGS TO LOOK FOR IN THE FUTURE**
- **THE UN-SUGARCOATED SUCKINESS YOU CAN EXPECT**
- **THE UNTRUE SUCKINESS YOU MUST REJECT**

Each chapter also has sidebars offering advice that's both funny and brutally honest. Two sidebars that appear in almost every chapter are:

DO MY FRIENDS OR PARENTS HAVE A POINT?

Parents get to have a say in all aspects of your life, from where you go to school to where you live to whether or not you might end up with the genes for obesity (thanks a lot, great-grandpa ironically known as "Tiny"). Friends, on the other hand, are expected to provide all manner of advice, on everything, all the time. That's why, when the people close to you try to control or just weigh in on more personal matters, it can sometimes feel like they're taking things one step too far.

Unfortunately, as much as it may seem like parental control should be limited, it can't be, because it's fueled by unlimited worry. Parents know that their actual ability to preserve your safety, future, and general well-being, despite all their efforts, is fairly weak. And while reliance on friends seems like it should be boundless, your friends' expertise is often as limited as your parents' concern is limitless. So before you greet every parental opinion with rolled eyes and every friend's opinion as gospel, read these breakdowns of what they're probably trying to say, no matter how unfair or clueless their actual words sound. Then you can decide whether their worries and criticisms are worth paying attention to or whether they're overreacting and you're eye-rolling just the right amount.

HOW TO BE AN ALLY

There are a few safe, reliable ways to help those in need, and many ways that trying to help can actually do harm. Your best approach for helping others is to think carefully about what you can do without taking on unnecessary responsibility and risk. That said, if you see someone who's hurting because of their differences, we list some things you can do, and some things you should avoid, if you want to help out.

So let's get on with discovering all the ways that life can suck, how you can accept it, and all the good things you can do about it from there.

CHAPTER ONE

FRIENDSHIP SUCKS

FOR MOST PEOPLE, IT'S HARD to imagine getting through life without friends. They're the ones we have the most fun with, who make us feel better when we're down, and who have our backs when bad people or big problems have us feeling cornered. Having friends seems like an important part of being a normal, happy person.

But if you don't have a lot of friends (or enough friends, or sometimes, any friends), your parents might worry that you're shy and uncomfortable around people your age, and your peers might think that there's something wrong with you.

Your peers might think that anyone who doesn't have lots of friends, or any friends, or has friends they don't approve of, is weird, or a loser, or a bunch of other negative, hurtful things that can make you feel even more friendless and alone.

If you have trouble making friends or want to be friends with people who don't want to be friends with you, it's easy to believe those negative, hurtful things. You might wonder if you're doing something wrong that makes it impossible for you to be likable. Which then might make you think the solution is to change yourself in order to find friends and get your parents and peers to think you're "normal."

The truth is that there are lots of reasons for not having friends, which you—or anyone else—can't control or change. You may be the sort of person who's more interested in spending time alone and maybe isn't worried about having friends right now. Or it could be that you just can't find anyone you want to be friends with. And you might not feel great about that, but it's okay.

Of course, you've probably watched lots of movies and TV shows where the "nerd" or "weirdo" gets a makeover or a magical best friend who impresses the cool kids and makes our nerdy hero into the king of the school. In real life, a new haircut just invites more teasing, and magical creatures are hard to find outside of fairy tales. Trying to fix the problem of friendlessness by changing yourself usually just makes you feel more helpless and lonely than you did to begin with.

That's why you shouldn't ever feel like making friends is what you're supposed to do, at least not until you've asked yourself whether making friends is possible and really better than spending more time alone.

Remember, being alone doesn't mean you have to be lonely, and it certainly doesn't mean that you're a loser. You're just making the best of not having friends for the time being, even if it means feeling lonely sometimes and having to listen to adults asking why you don't have friends. It means spending your time doing homework or reading or finding a hobby. And while you're doing that, if your school is truly a friend desert, you can keep an eye out for places outside of school where you might make friends, which can be anywhere from the library to a sports club to the local comic book shop.

And being alone or lonely should never push you to hang out with bad people and do bad things. Settling for the wrong friends, either because you think you need friends or because you want to make your parents happy, is just going to make everyone miserable. The wrong friends can tear down your confidence by not accepting you for who you are, or by dumping you when you need their support the most, or by getting you into trouble, or all of the above.

So when you feel friendless, not-friended-enough, or like a loser who's doomed to be alone, the answer isn't making friends by any means necessary or by doing something that makes other people, but not you, happy. The answer is to go slowly, figure out what you really need in a friend, and make friends only when you think they'll be good for you (while learning to spot bad friendship situations and stay away).

Don't let loneliness get you down when you can't help being lonely. Ignore the jerks at school, the doubting voice in your head, and even your worried parents, and be proud of yourself when you have good reasons for being friendless and aren't letting a bad situation or a load of bad luck get you down.

And when you do have friends around, accept that you

might not always get along. Getting through those rough patches is a good sign of how strong and worthwhile your friendship really is. Real friends stick with you, no matter how not-fun either one of you is to be around sometimes.

HOW TO FIGURE OUT FOR YOURSELF WHEN A FRIENDSHIP SUCKS:

The answers to many friendship problems depend on your own ideas of what makes a good friend and what makes a friendship worth having. Teachers, parents, and TV shows from the 1990s all have their own ideas of what kinds of friends you should have. But ultimately, it's up to you—not your PE teacher, your dad, or Ross and Rachel—to figure out your own standards of friendship. Here's a quiz to help you think about the things you should expect from a friend and from yourself as a friend. It will help you determine whether those expectations are reasonable or likely to cause trouble.

1 **You get so sick with some puketastic virus that you end up having to miss three days of school and have no contact with your friends. You expect your friends to:**
A) Totally freak out and organize a prayer vigil outside your house until you can hold down solid food.
B) Get in touch after the second day to find out what's going on and offer to come by to drop off homework or just say hi.
C) Not forget your name when you get back, but not much else.

2 You catch someone you considered a close friend telling your secrets to a bunch of kids who don't really like you, and they all share a good laugh. You decide to:

A) Fight fire with fire. Wait until everyone hears about that humiliating thing that happened to her last summer!

B) Calmly confront her about it later and see what she says—and if she denies it, don't fight, just give her space and stay guarded when she's around.

C) Laugh it off, because if you show you care then your friend will crank up the secret sharing.

3 A group of cool older kids have been asking you to hang out with them. While you're pretty sure they really like you, you don't feel comfortable saying no to them even when they want to do stuff that could get you grounded, arrested, or even dead. You decide to:

A) Tell them that the next time they try to pressure you into doing something bad, you're calling the cops, using a taser on them, or both.

B) Get brave, and politely turn down their next invite to join in their crazy adventure. And if they're not okay with it then it's time to find friends who aren't as exciting but are a lot less fake (and dangerous).

C) Ride out the adventure as long as you can and hope that if something does go wrong, you can stand the grounding and your parents can afford bail or funeral costs.

4 You and your best friend have known each other forever. You always have fun together and make each other

laugh. But you're starting to get into soccer and the two of you aren't spending as much time with each other, and you can tell she's not happy about that. Plus, your new soccer friends think she's weird. You decide to:

A) Force your soccer friends and your old friend to hang out with one another, even though it's awkward and your best friend never really has anything to say. It's the only way you can think of to make everybody happy, but it obviously makes everybody miserable.

B) Tell your old friend that you still value her friendship, despite your new interests, and make time to hang out with her. And make it clear to your new friends that if they're not cool with and to her, then you're not cool with them.

C) Tell your soccer friends you've ditched your old friend, but still secretly hang out with her, making sure your soccer friends don't see the two of you together. That way, again, everybody's happy (except you).

ANSWER KEY

IF YOUR ANSWERS WERE MAINLY As:

Your expectations are too high. You expect a lot from friendship, both from yourself and from others. You feel way too responsible for meeting impossible friendship standards, pushing so hard to "do the right thing" and protect your friends' feelings that you end up hurting their feelings and screwing up. And because you're so hard on yourself, you tend to punish others for not achieving your high standards. Unfortunately, friendships can easily be messed up by factors that nobody can control. So having high expectations and reacting impulsively to them is never smart, whether you're angry at a friend or angry at yourself. Instead of expecting people and friendships to be perfect, learn to think carefully about your right, and your friends' rights, to feel and do things that disappoint other people, at least in the short run, when there's no better alternative.

IF YOUR ANSWERS WERE MAINLY Bs:

Your expectations are just right. You're getting the hang of being kind to others while also paying attention to your own needs (also known as being a good friend to other people and to yourself). Overall, you know how to be a good friend and good person, even if, like every human being, you don't always do the best job of it. You accept the fact that feelings change in ways you can't control and that people aren't perfect. Some friendships stop working, some people will let you down, and you may disappoint some people. But it usually won't do you any good to force relationships to be something they are not or to punish other people or yourself. Instead, learn to accept uncontrollable changes in a friendship while becoming more selective about who you spend time with, even if it means going slowly and being lonely sometimes. A good friend is someone you can trust and rely on, and people like that aren't easy to find.

IF YOUR ANSWERS WERE MAINLY Cs:

Your expectations are too low. You're not willing to put in the effort to make potential friendships work if they seem too risky or "uncool." But you are too willing to forgive and tolerate bad friends without protecting yourself from being hurt or mistreated. Friendship isn't always fun and often requires work, but that's how life is in general. The point of friendship isn't just having people in your life whose support and understanding make it easier to get through life's ups and downs, but also being that person to others. So, in order to make good friends and avoid bad friends, raise your standards for being a good friend. And expect good friendship from the people you hang out with. It's not worth it to compromise.

DO MY PARENTS HAVE A POINT?

WHEN YOUR PARENTS SAY . . .

"That friend of yours is [insert difference here]—I don't want them in my house."

IT SOUNDS DUMB BECAUSE . . .

They're being total bigots, and there's no defending their Jurassic-era attitudes toward people who are different.

BUT IT'S NOT DUMB TO THEM BECAUSE . . .

They may be scared or ignorant—that's not to say what they've said is okay, but that their worries, as misplaced and wrong as they may be, could come from a place of love and concern for you.

SO BE SMART AND . . .

Remember that some adults have ideas about

acceptance that are just plain outdated and wrong. And responding to them with anger, while justified, won't do much to bring their ideas up to date.

THEN RESPOND BY . . .

Telling them that you know they're trying to protect you, but that they shouldn't let your friend's race, religion, gender identity, or any other attribute distract them from the true quality of your friend's character.

FRIENDSHIP SUCKS . . .

When Your Friendship Isn't Working

WHEN A FRIEND SUDDENLY DOESN'T feel like a friend anymore, it can make you feel confused at best and totally crappy at worst. But sometimes it's hard to understand why things aren't right, especially if no one's done anything wrong. So, when what seemed like a good friendship starts to make either one of you feel bad, as difficult as it may be, you need to figure out what, if anything, went wrong. That way you'll know whether things can be made right or if you even want them to go back to the way they were.

HERE'S AN EXAMPLE:

I never thought the cool guys would want to hang out with me. But they do now that I've gotten good at basketball, and it's pretty awesome. They're the ones at school who make everyone laugh and always have the best time. I'm worried, though, because some of the fun stuff they like to do is not cool with me. But if I act shocked or say I don't want to join in then I'll be out of the group entirely and they (and everyone else) will make fun of me for being a dork and a loser. And I like being part of their group otherwise, so maybe I *am* just being a dork. I need to figure out how to stay in with these guys without getting into trouble or becoming their number one target.

SIGNS YOU MAY BE MISINTERPRETING THINGS:

They claim that when they give you a hard time for avoiding doing stuff with them that they're not really mad, just joking around. Which would be easier to believe if their joking was more funny than mean.

. . . AND SIGNS YOU AREN'T:

This new group of friends have been cruel to people in the past who haven't fallen in line with them and their expectations of what it takes to stay in the group.

WHAT YOUR PARENTS SAY TO TRY TO HELP:

"Just be yourself and your friends will like you for you," or "Maybe if you try harder to involve them in the things you like to do, they won't always push you to do what they want to do."

. . . AND WHY IT ISN'T HELPFUL AT ALL:

They're your parents, so your safety, your future, and your overall happiness are their priority, not your possible status as king or queen. If you follow their advice, you might meet their goals of staying out of jail, avoiding jerks, and focusing on your own interests, but you'll have to live through a banishment to the kingdom of misery first.

WHAT YOU THINK YOU NEED TO FIGURE OUT IN ORDER TO FIX IT:

Find a way to go along with your friends' risky or annoying behavior while still keeping yourself safe and sane. Or make a plan for becoming so likable and cool that you'll be able to suggest any activity and they'll go along with you.

WHY THOSE FIXES WILL FAIL:

Any time you push yourself to do something that doesn't feel right, you'll like yourself less for being a wimp. And since it's really hard to pretend to be someone you aren't for very long, your friends will like you less because the only thing worse than a wimp is a fake. You can't stop your friends from liking to do the wrong things, liking you for the wrong reasons, or not liking the person you're becoming. And you can't hide the effort you're making to fit in, or the fact that you're not actually the kind of person who meets their standards of cool (because, in fact, you think their standards are pretty stupid and annoying anyway).

WHAT YOU CAN ACTUALLY DO ABOUT IT:

Ask people whose judgment you trust (who can include your parents) about the situation you're in. Explain what you think might be a good solution. Once you've had that conversation, do what you think is right, which will probably involve staying away from situations that will put you at risk. Yes, taking a stand could put you at risk of being teased or possibly shunned. Someone's nasty reaction may be upsetting, but when you know you're doing right by yourself, you don't have to defend yourself or compromise yourself in order to gain approval. It's better to accept who you are, even if others don't think you're cool or popular, than accept the abuse and compromise that comes with trying to be someone you aren't.

RED FLAGS TO LOOK FOR IN THE FUTURE:

Avoid people who only want to be friends on their terms—terms that require you to make big compromises for them that don't feel right, or may even be dangerous. Especially if they aren't putting in any effort or making compromises themselves. Also, be wary of people who may be friendly to you but enjoy being mean to others, because if you join in their cruelty in order to keep their friendship, you could be their next target.

THE UN-SUGARCOATED SUCKINESS YOU CAN EXPECT:

Everyone makes bad friends sometimes, and if you have to "break up" with them, it sucks, even if it's the right thing to do. After all, even if they were crappy friends worth losing, you'll still miss the fun you once had. Especially if you now spend most of your time alone and feel like a sad loser. And sometimes there's the risk of being bullied for being friendless.

THE UNTRUE SUCKINESS YOU MUST REJECT:

It's hard when the people you once thought of as cool turn out to be the opposite. But don't believe the voices, whether they come from bullies or your own brain, that tell you that you're a loser, or a reject, or any label that implies that you deserve to feel this way and always will. You know you tried to be friendly while not bending your own standards to make the cool kids like you, and that takes great strength. If those friendships disappear as people get to know the real you, you're better off without them. Don't think you're suffering because you did something wrong.

Boundaries 101: Knowing When to Share Secrets Online and When to Shut Up Instead

Learning what personal information is safe to share with whom—that is, how to develop and maintain "personal boundaries"—is a difficult process that humans have struggled with for ages, even before Alexander Graham Bell invented the telephone.

He's just lucky he didn't have to deal with social media. Now, of course, you must assume that every word and image you put online or in an email or text can be seen by anyone, up to and including your crush, the admissions department of your dream college, and/or your local police department.

So before you post something online that you know could cause drama with someone, ask yourself three questions: (1) Would I say or show this to this person face-to-face? (2) Or to a group of people? (3) Even if that group was made up of strangers who will judge me based only on what I'm about to say or show?

You may feel like self-censoring means being untrue to yourself since you're hiding your deepest feelings, but if your true self is someone who wants to be a fair, kind, and overall good person, then you can't do worse than presenting the angriest, meanest, and most emotional version of yourself online as who you really are. Communication may have evolved way beyond the telephone, but that doesn't mean you should use it to embarrass or hurt others or yourself.

FRIENDSHIP SUCKS . . .
When Your Friends Are Acting Like Jerks

FRIENDS ARE THE ONES YOU'RE supposed to turn to when you're stumped by a problem, but when a friend *is* the problem, you can be left feeling twice as lost. After all, if your friend is acting like a jerk, then there's no one around to help you figure out what can be done. The good news, though—which is also the bad news— is that, in those situations, there's probably nothing that can be done, especially if you've already tried talking it out. Friendships do sometimes unravel for no clear reason, which means there's no easy fix to the problem and there's nothing you're supposed to do. What's important at that point is not to find a way to feel better or stay friends, but to develop your ability to tell whether you or the friend has done something wrong. Decide whether your friendship, no matter how much you depend on it and want it to continue, and regardless of how angry or hurt you're feeling, is worth losing for good.

HERE'S AN EXAMPLE:

I'm lucky to have had a best friend since third grade who's always had my back. But a month ago she started to avoid me in the halls and ignore my texts, and I couldn't figure out why. I asked her if something was up, and she acted like I must be joking because she thought everything was normal. So I figured if anything was really wrong it would just blow over quickly. Instead, it seems to be getting worse. She barely sits with me at lunch now (and acts annoyed when she does) and never wants to make plans. And when I try to get her to just tell me what the problem is, she tells me I'm being crazy over nothing and stressing her out, and that's the only problem here. I want to figure out what I did wrong, or what's wrong, period, so I can save our friendship.

SIGNS YOU MAY BE MISINTERPRETING THINGS:

Everyone goes through blue periods where the way they think about and see the world is twisted. It's easy to get down on yourself when you're going through a blue period. You can't believe that anyone really wants to be around someone as uncool and pathetic as you are, and you've stopped trusting your friends and even teachers and your parents. And you can't help but kind of hate everything. Feeling like this sucks, but there are things you can do to make it stop so it's definitely worth talking about the way you feel with someone you trust.

. . . AND SIGNS YOU AREN'T:

If you don't feel down in general and you've counted up the times your friend didn't text when she said she would, and your other friends have noticed that something between you two seems off, then you've got proof that this isn't in your head. Your instinct may be to explain away your friend's bad behavior rather than accept the pain of loss and betrayal. But doing that will just make you nuts. At this point, you'll need to accept that the friendship is over—at least for now. And that sucks, but it's better to accept it than go down the rabbit hole of doubt.

WHAT YOUR PARENTS SAY TO TRY TO HELP:

"Maybe you're being too sensitive," or "Just be your usual self and she'll get over it," or "Just tell her what she's doing that's hurting you because I'm sure once she knows, she'll stop."

. . . AND WHY IT ISN'T HELPFUL AT ALL:

You've probably already attempted to talk with your friend and gotten nothing but denials and defensive remarks in return. So you know you're not making it up. Plus you've already tried being every version of yourself—normal, super nice, extra-assertive—and for some infuriating, painful, mysterious reason, your friend still wants nothing to do with any of them.

WHAT YOU THINK YOU NEED TO FIGURE OUT IN ORDER TO FIX IT:

If you could just find a way to make it clear to your friend how much you care and how she's making you feel, she'd finally see your point. She would sympathize with your hurt and frustration, apologize, feel comfortable talking to you about what's bothering her, and promise to change.

WHY THOSE FIXES WILL FAIL:

If, up to this point, you haven't been able to get your friend to admit what she's doing, to agree that you have a right to be upset, and to show that she's sorry and wants to change, then you probably never will. It's possible she's not even sure what's bothering her, or she feels she's just reacting to something you're doing. The idea that you're upset means she'll want to avoid you or prove that your unhappiness is all your fault. No matter what's going on in her head, it's clear by now that it's not something you should expect to figure out or fix.

WHAT YOU CAN ACTUALLY DO ABOUT IT
(WHETHER YOU'RE READY TO GIVE UP ON YOUR FRIENDSHIP OR NOT):

If you've done everything a good friend should to try to save your friendship—admitted any fault on your side and apologized, tried to address any fault on her side in a calm and constructive way—and you still can't make things right, then it's time to accept that the friendship is over. Once you know that doing your best isn't good enough, doing more is your worst option. Trying to make things right focuses your thoughts on how awful it feels to be rejected or treated badly. It pushes you into second-guessing, doubt-filled thoughts. Never let someone else's behavior, even your former best friend's, control the way you judge your own actions and live your own life.

Respect your efforts, patience, and willingness to accept any deserved blame, then stop doubting yourself. And it doesn't mean retaliating against your old friend or closing the door on regaining her friendship. But it does mean that, because of the way she treated you, it will take a lot to win back your trust and friendship.

RED FLAGS TO LOOK FOR IN THE FUTURE:

Some people are easy to get close to and have fun with. But if they don't give you as much as you give them, get over hurt feelings in a reasonable amount of time, or accept you when things aren't easy or fun—then beware. They're showing you that they don't have the stuff required to maintain a friendship that lasts. They can't really be relied on or trusted as a good friend. But before you even get to that point, ask yourself how reliable they've been to other friends, or whether they've bounced around from group to group over the past couple of years. If you look for red flags before getting too close, you can protect yourself from a lot of hurt, loss, and self-doubt.

THE UN-SUGARCOATED SUCKINESS YOU CAN EXPECT:

When a close friendship starts to fall apart, especially when there's no obvious reason, there's often no clear or easy way to solve the problem. If it's a misunderstanding or something one of you can apologize for, that's a relatively easy fix. But too often the problem is something more complicated because it comes from something that you or your friend can't see or change, or maybe even understand and describe. That leaves you with all the hurt that comes from losing a friend, as well as the doubt and anger that come from not knowing why or knowing that her reason is unfair. If you're not careful, you can also lose a great deal of self-confidence.

THE UNTRUE SUCKINESS YOU MUST REJECT:

It's easy to believe the worst about yourself when you're feeling down. But no matter how much you find yourself hurting and doubting yourself, don't let this experience make you believe that you can't ever trust what you see in a friendship. Don't blame yourself because your friend dumped you and it's hard to believe she'd do that without a good reason. This might feel like the right conclusion when you're down on yourself, but take a moment to think about the kind of person you are. You'll most likely realize that, no matter how little confidence you have right now, the facts about your character, actions, and who you are tell a different story. That's why you must trust your own way of figuring out what happened, judging whether or not you're to blame and need to apologize, and making smarter, educated choices about whom to be friends with in the future.

Loving Your Loner Status— How to Embrace Being an Outsider (Without Being an A-hole), by S.B.

As you may already know by now, there are some people, including yours truly, who, for one reason or another, are never going to be considered "cool." At a certain point, almost every outsider comes to terms with her status. Unfortunately, acceptance rarely brings what the art teachers who like to wear a lot of silver jewelry and sandals might call "inner peace." For me, being okay with being weird didn't mean feeling happy and proud; instead, I was resentful and pissed.

That's because, after so many years of not being approved of or included by the kings and queens of the class (and being mocked by them for the same), it's easy for anyone to hit their breaking point and go from being hurt to being angry. From there, outcasts often accept their weirdo status with pride, but turn things around by openly rejecting and mocking the cooler kids, the whole idea of coolness, and/or the overall social status quo.

On the one hand, being proud of who you are, especially when that differs from the established, arbitrary guidelines of "normal," isn't just an acceptable thing to do, but an admirable one. On the other hand, living your truth shouldn't be more important than living up to your values; being your true weirdo self shouldn't eclipse your greater goal of being a good person. Especially if being your own person is defined by risky behavior or a nasty, reactionary attitude to the very people you don't want to be defined by in the first place.

In other words, if embracing individuality means being sarcastic, creative, and loud, then there's no reason to hold back, as long as you stay true to your values and priorities. So don't start doing things that make it hard to live up to your expectations for what it means to be a good friend, kid, or human being in general. Accepting loner status doesn't mean you have to become unfriendly, nasty, and/or bitter, because then you're not defining yourself by your own terms and standards but by the ways others perceive you. It shouldn't matter that they don't get you or wouldn't be friends with you because, if you like what you're doing just fine, their reaction to you shouldn't dictate your reaction to them.

Feeling angry with the people who reject you is natural, but it's also an unnecessary distraction. If they don't want your friendship, they don't deserve any extra brain space. I could have been myself without being so hostile to people

I was certain were judging me since I (a): was just being paranoid and (b): shouldn't have cared what they thought in the first place. So if you're ready to accept outsider status, be careful to do so on your terms. You may be doing it out of hurt and anger, but anger doesn't and shouldn't define who you are.

FRIENDSHIP SUCKS . . .

When You Don't Have Friends, Period

WHEN YOU DON'T HAVE FRIENDS—or even worse, when you seem to have lots of enemies—it's almost impossible not to feel like a bit of a loser. Unfortunately, we usually feel this way because "loner = loser" in this world. But there's also something in our brains, in the part we share with other social mammals, that tells us that being part of a herd is crucial to our survival. Since that part of our brain also tells us to be afraid of the dark and that fighting is okay,

it's wise not to believe everything your brain says. Lots of people don't have an easy time making friends, while many jerks somehow excel at it. And it's not impossible to be a good, interesting, friend-worthy person who lives a fun and interesting life, even if you have to spend some of it alone. Do try to make friends and generally respect your social animal instincts. But don't assume that there's something wrong with you if you can't make friendships happen. Loneliness can be hard, but being alone doesn't have to be.

HERE'S AN EXAMPLE:

I don't know why my classmates don't like me. They hardly ever talk to me, and when they do, a lot of the time it's just something mean, anyway. I thought it was because I'm shy, but when I've pushed myself to talk to people who seem friendly, it still doesn't work. My parents are worried because they see I'm alone. They keep encouraging me to make friends, but it's hard. Needless to say, school isn't much fun. If I knew what I was doing wrong, I'd change it.

SIGNS YOU MAY BE MISINTERPRETING THINGS:

As we explained in the previous section, when you're feeling down, your brain can play fast and loose with the facts. So there may be a couple of people you can hang out with, but the feeling that you're a loser prevents you from recognizing and remembering that and welcoming them. So if you're in a state of mind where you're just seeing the world through brown-colored glasses, you may be seeing a crappy situation where there isn't one.

. . . AND SIGNS YOU AREN'T:

You've tried very hard to be friendly and make friends, but the result is always disappointing.

WHAT YOUR PARENTS SAY TO TRY TO HELP:

"You've just got to give it time and give them more of a chance," or "Maybe you just have to get a better idea of what their wavelength is, then you can get onto it," or "You made friends before, there's no reason you can't make friends now."

. . . AND WHY IT ISN'T HELPFUL AT ALL:

You've given other kids plenty of chances, but they won't give you one, no matter how hard you've tried to get on their "wavelength." Long story short, you've tried your parents' suggestions and they haven't worked. But they keep saying that you can succeed if you really want to, which just makes you feel like more of a failure.

WHAT YOU THINK YOU NEED TO FIGURE OUT IN ORDER TO FIX IT:

Something—like the kind of motivational pep talk somebody usually gives to the hero near the end of a feel-good movie—that will give you the confidence or social savvy to end your current loserhood forever.

WHY THOSE FIXES WILL FAIL:

Because this is real life and not a movie, and you can't magically change the way other people think. Instead of thinking too much about ways to have a social life, it's time to work on ways to be okay with the not-social life you've got.

WHAT YOU CAN ACTUALLY DO ABOUT IT:

Instead of filling your solo time longing for friends to hang out with, focus on yourself, pursue your own hobbies, and think about the qualities that any future friend must have. So maybe you start running or building robots, and then find ways to make new friends through those interests by signing up for local races and meeting people to train with or joining a district-wide robot team. Keep being a good person while refusing to be defined by kids who don't want to be friends with you or don't have the character to be reliable friends. Have faith that friendship will come at some point, and that you can handle doing things on your own until it does.

RED FLAGS TO LOOK FOR IN THE FUTURE:

Beware of groups that focus on having stuff (sneakers, clothes, phones) rather than being stuff (kind, honest, reliable). Friends should be less interested in the exact make and model of sneakers and more interested in the personality of the sneaker wearer. Also, beware of groups that are less interested in positive activities, whether that's playing sports or speaking Klingon, and more interested in negative ones, like finding someone to torment or something to destroy. And anyone you have to work really hard to win over isn't worth the effort.

THE UN-SUGARCOATED SUCKINESS YOU CAN EXPECT:

You can expect to be spending time on your own, as well as getting some crap from people who think that makes you pretty sad, but if the way to avoid those jerks is even more time on your own, then so be it.

THE UNTRUE SUCKINESS YOU MUST REJECT:

Just because you might have bad luck when it comes to making friends doesn't mean that you're a bad person who nobody will ever want to be around. Don't confuse having no friends with having no worth or no future, no matter what the voices in or outside of your head say. Not having friends can make life hard, but don't let that distract you from the important day-to-day stuff, like learning what you can in school and being good to those you do care about. Ultimately, you have to learn to stay focused and sane by being a good friend to yourself.

HOW TO BE AN ALLY . . .

TO SOMEONE WITH FRIEND PROBLEMS

THE PROBLEM:

Two of your friends are fighting—Friend A doesn't understand why, and Friend B is too angry to talk to her.

WHAT YOU WANT TO DO:

Lock A and B together in a room, car, or toilet stall until they work it out; insist you all sit down together so you can negotiate peace; work as an intermediary and negotiate peace on the sly.

. . . AND WHY YOU SHOULDN'T:

Neither one of them has taken responsibility for making peace, so they're just blaming each other for being bad friends. If you try to intervene, they may just turn their anger on you. Then they may fight with each other less, but shaft you altogether.

WHAT YOU CAN DO:

The next time either friend tries to talk to you about the fight, ask them about whether the good part of their friendship is more important than the bad feelings they're experiencing at the moment. And if so, whether they'd be willing to focus on the good and meet to talk things out.

FRIENDS SUCK: THE POINT

Staying in a bad friendship just to avoid being alone is so much worse than being alone and lonely. It's important not to just think about what you *need* friendship for, but what you want from a friend and a friendship. Think about the qualities you admire in other people that have to do with their actions, not the impression they make. For example, whether they are accepting and relatable, not whether they always have the coolest footwear or sit at the best lunch table. If things get rough, remember that good friends can sometimes act like jerks and jerks can sometimes seem like good friends, so the tough times are worth it since they're the only sure way of learning how to tell friends and jerks apart. Having a friend turn on you may suck, but that's when you must decide for yourself whether a jerky friend is really a good person and worth keeping or whether a friend you really care about is bad for you and needs to be dropped. And when there are no possible friends around, that's when you think about what you want from yourself, not just as a friend but as an individual. Find the strength to pursue your own goals, accomplish what's important to you, and stay true to the only loyal company you'll always have in your life—yourself.

CHAPTER TWO

SCHOOL SUCKS

IN ORDER TO ENCOURAGE YOU and give you strong self-esteem, parents tell you that if you approach school with a good, positive attitude and a willingness to work, participate in extracurriculars, and trust that school will be fair and safe, you'll be rewarded with "the best years of your life." What they fail to realize, however, is that their positive encouragement and good intentions may be setting you up to blame yourself if bad luck tosses you into a scenario where nothing goes right.

Adults tend to romanticize their school days. They can forget how school is real work, because it's actually a job. It's a job that takes up most of your waking hours, tests you constantly, and sometimes forces you to share hours, if not years, with horrible "coworkers" and unfair "bosses."

For some, school is a great job they enjoy, work hard at, and get fulfilling rewards from. For others, however, school isn't so much a fair, challenging job as a constant, unjust punishment. It feels like a series of dead-end tasks no matter how hard you work and try to stay positive. And if you have to deal with things totally out of your control, such as learning difficulties or challenging life circumstances, it can be extremely hard for your brain to absorb or process new information. When you can't get the promised good grades, friends, or fun out of school, even if it's because your brain is allergic to focusing, or your classmates seem allergic to you, or you're just allergic to schoolwork, period, those uncontrollable issues feel like personal failures.

Working hard is always worthwhile, even when it doesn't pay off in the way you expected. But if you find yourself working hard and getting nowhere, then it could be that you've run into an unsolvable problem that you don't deserve. But just because a problem is uncontrollable or unsolvable doesn't mean it's hopeless. Nor does it mean you caused the problem and deserve that burden. It just means these particular issues can't be resolved, even by your trying harder or improving your attitude. Believing that they can will make you feel even more out of control.

Even if you can learn to manage impossible problems, that doesn't necessarily mean you'll discover the way to good grades or happiness. Sometimes the good results won't show up until much later, or the resulting grades won't be good, just better, or—and this is the toughest and most important result to appreciate—the only good result will be your knowledge that you're doing the right thing. That's not as satisfying as an A or an invitation to hang out with the cool kids, but when you make the bottom line getting through school (or any other difficult situation) without compromising the kind of person you want to be, it's a much bigger achievement.

Learning how to cope when life gets in the way of your ambitions and remaining a good, hardworking, independent person is the most important thing you can learn, in school or anywhere else.

HOW TO FIGURE OUT FOR YOURSELF WHEN SCHOOL SUCKS:

We all rely on grades to let us know how we're doing in school. But grades don't tell the whole story, especially if you're dealing with factors such as difficulties with learning, with your family, or with certain teachers. Besides, grades reflect test scores and the quality of your homework, and don't necessarily take into account the quality of your effort. As important as it is to get good grades, it's more important to work hard and be a good person, whether that affects your report card or not. Here's a quiz to help you think about how you deal with school life.

1 This coming Thursday night marks two major events—the last chance to study for your French final and the midnight premiere of the movie that you've been waiting for all year. If you focus on the final, you'll probably do well, but you'll have to skip the special screening. If you go to the screening and skip studying, you'll do okay on the final, but not your best. You decide to:

A) Go to the movie, because if you go and skip studying, you still won't fail the class. But if you don't go and study instead, you'll miss a guaranteed night of awesomeness, which everyone else but you will be talking about on Friday morning.

B) Either find a way to fit in some extra studying or accept the fact that you're just going to have to wait to see the movie another time. You've been working too hard in this class all year to settle for a mediocre final grade that doesn't reflect your efforts.

C) You would never risk going to a movie on a school night, let alone the night before a final, so you've accepted that you probably won't see it until it's finally available on demand.

2 After writing three drafts, meeting with the teacher, and getting help from your parents, you managed to get a B+ on your final history paper. But your genius best friend put off writing and even researching the paper until the night before it was due, and she still managed to get an A. From this, it's clear to you that:

A) Duh, she's a genius, and duh, you're a dumbass, so no matter how much work you put in, you'll never measure up to your friend.

B) She is truly a magical unicorn student. And while you're in awe (and openly jealous) of her powers, you know that your inability to crank out A papers like she can doesn't mean that there's something wrong with you. It's just one thing that's crazy right with her.

C) Go to the teacher and ask for an opportunity to do rewrites or get extra credit. Then make your friend swear on her GPA that her A didn't happen by magic—or some other strange occurrence, because you will not rest until you get to the bottom of this travesty and the grade you rightly deserve.

3 Everyone's on your case about getting your grade up in physics. But it's been hard for you to apply yourself because you hate math and science so much and have zero skills in those subjects. So every time you sit down to do your homework, you resolve to:

A) Continue coming up with any answers as quickly as possible so you can get back to doing literally anything else. Handing in some answers, even if they're wrong, is better than doing what you really want with the homework, which is using it as toilet paper.

B) Find someone—a science-savvy friend, a parent, or the teacher— to sit down with you and work through some of the questions together. They will help you figure things out, but, just as important, their spending time with you will force you to focus and make an effort.

C) Tape your eyeballs open so you can give the material 100 percent of your focus, understand 100 percent of the material, and get 100 percent on your final grade.

4 You knocked yourself out to get a B in your weakest class, Spanish. Your parents made it clear to you that they were expecting you to get an A, and they don't just mean in effort. You respond by:

A) Telling them it was a miracle you got a B. And, given their disappointed response, they shouldn't "B" surprised if you stop making any effort in *el futuro*.

B) Doing your best to stay calm while explaining that, for whatever reason, Spanish is never going to be a subject you ace. You're certain of this because you absolutely gave the class your best effort and have a B to show for it. So they can either grumble over the fact that you didn't get an A or be happy that you did as *bien* as you did.

C) Making it clear to them that you were also expecting an A, hate yourself for falling short of everyone's expectations, and are generally *mucho más* disappointed in yourself than they could ever be.

IF YOUR ANSWERS WERE MAINLY As:

Your expectations are too low. You probably avoid thinking much about grades, get discouraged or distracted easily, and aren't particularly fazed by poor results and a teacher's criticism. You may not think that school is worth it, at least in terms of the subjects you're learning. However, the most important things you learn in school aren't just the quadratic equation or who won the War of 1812. School also teaches you how to keep at it despite some tedious and unpleasant circumstances. And that's an invaluable survival skill. Instead, what you're doing is training yourself to ignore the worry and self-doubt that go with caring. It may make you happy now, but it will also stop you from gaining confidence in your own toughness and discovering the pride of doing your best.

IF YOUR ANSWERS WERE MAINLY Bs:

Your expectations are just right. You don't let trying to get good grades get in the way of being a thoughtful person and a good friend. You accept your strengths and weaknesses, and know how to judge your own personal performance. You always give your best effort, whether trying hard is unlikely to get a good result or barely trying is likely to be good enough. You may often feel pulled in several directions as you try to keep your grades up while also trying to have a life, but that just means you're doing things right.

IF YOUR ANSWERS WERE MAINLY Cs:

Your expectations are too high. Your obsession with good grades has taken over your life and crowded out other important values, like friendship and developing nonacademic skills. Academic success may temporarily make you feel good and worthy, but only until you realize there's another test or paper right around the corner. You hate seeing someone do better than you, particularly if they don't work as hard. And you live with the fear of doing badly. But unless you can find a way to balance your ambition for good grades with being a good person, you'll never be truly satisfied.

Defining "Dumb"

Dumb, like *awesome* or *literally*, is one of those words that is used frequently but is frequently used wrong. You may beat yourself up for being dumb if you fail a math test despite studying really hard. Or you may call someone else dumb as an insult for not knowing how to pass in hockey. But neither of those examples is a literal example of being dumb (and that's using *literal* in the correct sense).

Not being good at something isn't the same as being dumb. After all, lots of very smart people are terrible with numbers, and many academic types don't know the first thing about team sports. Therefore, it's not reasonable to use *dumb* to describe someone who's demonstrated a lack of talent in one or several areas, or to describe an action that's subpar.

It's definitely not reasonable to describe yourself as dumb if you're not very strong in some subjects, especially if it's despite your best efforts. The healthier approach is to accept that you have certain areas of weakness. That's not to say that you should give up trying to do well at anything that doesn't come naturally to you, but to adjust your approach, as well as your expectations. It's better to acknowledge your weaknesses and search for new ways to manage them rather than to push yourself repeatedly toward perfection. Don't call yourself stupid when you fall short.

Even if you get better results by carefully managing your approach toward problem subjects, those results will probably fall short of the ones you'd get in other, easier areas. But it's far more satisfying to get okay grades after working crazy hard on a subject that's especially difficult for you than it is to get great ones in a subject you can effortlessly ace.

As far as *dumb* is concerned, it should only really be used to describe something if it's purposely destructive, amoral, or unwise. Even then, it's not accurate to describe someone who does something dumb as dumb themselves, because even smart people make big mistakes for reasons that aren't immediately obvious. Plus, the whole "no name calling" thing you were taught in kindergarten still applies.

So don't be quick to call yourself or anyone else dumb, but be mindful of acknowledging where your talents lie, and avoid doing dumb things. Then, no matter what you're good at, you'll be doing an *awesome* (not exactly) job of being a good person.

SECTION 1

SCHOOL SUCKS . . .

When You're Working Really Hard
but Get Sucky Results

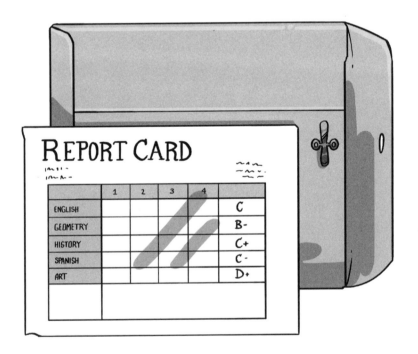

YOU WANT YOUR HARD WORK at school to pay off. And when it comes to achieving those goals, parents often give conflicting advice (cribbed from the music they listened to when they were your age). One day they might say, "You can't always get what you want." And the next day they promise that "you can get it if you really want, but you must try, try and try." All you really want is the truth, and that lies somewhere in between the two. So the key is to find a better way to manage yourself and your thoughts when hard work doesn't get you the desired results. With the right perspective and drive, you may not get what you want, but you can still succeed "at last."

HERE'S AN EXAMPLE:

I know I'm pretty smart, but at my supercompetitive high school where everyone is expected to go to college, I work really hard and still never seem to get good grades. It's really frustrating to bust my ass for average grades and still get criticism from my parents and teachers. In the meantime, it's not like I have nothing going for me, college-wise—I'm on two varsity sports teams and get solos in orchestra. I would feel better, or at least less down about it, if anyone acknowledged those talents (or anything but my failures). As it stands, I'm just getting discouraged and my self-esteem is being destroyed. I want to succeed, but if hard work isn't the key to making that happen then at least I want to feel less miserable.

SIGNS YOU MAY BE MISINTERPRETING THINGS:

Some people push themselves so hard that they don't hear the positive things that people say about them. So maybe you're writing off all the good feedback or support you get, both for your efforts and your other skills, because you're too focused on the obstacles you face and the ways you fall short.

. . . AND SIGNS YOU AREN'T:

You've thought about how well you do or don't do relative to your brainpower or potential, and it's clear that classmates who aren't smarter get better grades while appearing to put in a fraction of the work you do. Plus, everyone seems to want to focus on your failures rather than your successes.

WHAT YOUR PARENTS SAY TO TRY TO HELP:

"Everyone knows you're smart, so it's time to do whatever it takes to let your grades reflect who you really are!" or "Good grades are a reflection of hard work and making good choices, so if you're willing to do those things, voilà, straight As," or "If only you had a better attitude, your grades would improve."

. . . AND WHY IT ISN'T HELPFUL AT ALL:

Of course your parents mean well, but it's really irritating to be told you're lazy or uncaring when you couldn't try harder if your life depended on it. And being told to get more organized or less distracted does nothing to reduce your workload, change your life situation, or change the behavior of the people distracting you. And it certainly does nothing to improve your self-esteem.

WHAT YOU THINK YOU NEED TO FIGURE OUT IN ORDER TO FIX IT:

You want to find out exactly what's preventing your success, despite all your hard work, and resolve it. Or maybe just figure out how other people get good grades with a bit less effort and/or a million other things going on.

WHY THOSE FIXES WILL FAIL:

You might be happier if things were easier, but then you wouldn't be developing the strength and discipline you'll need next month, next year, and for the rest of your life. You also can't change your personality, and you may or may not be able to reduce the activities that limit your studying time. But the problem with your parents' advice also applies to the proposed solutions previously described. If you know you've reached the limit of what you can control but keep pushing yourself harder, it will just make your situation worse instead of better.

WHAT YOU CAN ACTUALLY DO ABOUT IT:

You can't let your negative feelings cause you to doubt your values or priorities. Coaches, parents, and motivational posters with kittens on them may tell you that you can overcome any obstacle if you try hard enough. In reality, however, the goal with obstacles that you know you can't overcome is to accept them and figure out ways to manage and work around them. Your goal in school is to figure out how to learn as much as you can despite the problems that interfere with your learning, regardless of whether you get praise or prestige. Whether your hurdle is being bad at taking tests, needing more study time, or having to deal with crap from bullies, what counts is not getting great results but doing the right thing when great results aren't possible. And that includes looking for ways to improve your results by talking to a trusted teacher, adviser, or your parents about changing your schedule so you can fit in all your activities, or asking the teacher whose class is really stumping you for help. Regardless of whether or not your grades improve, be proud of yourself for trying to do what's important and right despite dealing with a tough, unavoidable, and possibly painful situation. If you've taught yourself how to do that, you've aced the toughest test that life will throw at you.

RED FLAGS TO LOOK FOR IN THE FUTURE:

In order to avoid letting your situation at school overwhelm you, don't compare your grades or performance to your classmates'. At the same time, though, don't isolate yourself from your teachers or your classmates because you're embarrassed by your grades or just want to avoid the topic. Avoiding grade talk is as bad as being obsessed with it. Don't take shortcuts by choosing courses that teach you nothing new over ones that cover material you're genuinely interested in. Most importantly, never ever assume that being unhappy or getting bad grades always means you're doing the wrong thing. Getting bad grades doesn't mean you're failing as a person.

THE UN-SUGARCOATED SUCKINESS YOU CAN EXPECT:

Unfortunately, people will continue to get on your case about your grades. They may also fail to recognize your effort, ability, or obstacles, which will likely leave you frustrated, and perhaps humiliated. You may not be able to avoid disappointment or resentment at someone else's ability to learn more easily than you do. You may sometimes feel helpless due to your inability to manage all the activities, jobs, or jerks life throws your way. But no matter how much it hurts to try and fail, remember that learning is going to be important all your life. School is only the beginning, and staying curious and working hard to keep learning are the things that matter most and always deserve respect.

THE UNTRUE SUCKINESS YOU MUST REJECT:

When you're held to particularly high academic standards, the stakes also feel pretty high. You're often made to believe that if you don't get As then you won't get into a good college, which means you won't get a good job, which means you'll die penniless and alone with nothing written on your gravestone except "LOSER." However, don't feel like you have to keep pushing yourself or you'll be throwing your life away. There are great futures out there for good people who work hard, even if they don't have the greatest grades to show for it.

DO MY PARENTS HAVE A POINT?

WHEN YOUR PARENTS SAY . . .

"That you're so good at [art/science/English] proves that you would do as well in other subjects if you just tried harder."

IT SOUNDS DUMB BECAUSE . . .

Being good at one thing doesn't mean you're good at everything; nobody expects an NFL quarterback to also be an Olympic skier and a published poet. That's absurd, and instead of motivating you to work harder, it just makes you feel like a failure.

BUT IT'S NOT DUMB TO THEM BECAUSE . . .

They see your success as a result of hard work and talent. So if you have the talent and ability to work hard enough to do well in one area, then they figure, correctly or not, that you should be able to transfer those skills to other areas that you may not like as much.

SO BE SMART AND . . .

Think about whether you're really working as hard as you can in the areas that don't come as easily to you.

If you aren't, then aim to push yourself harder. But if you are doing your best, then believe in your own self-assessment and talk to your teachers and parents about figuring out strategies for making studying more effective.

THEN RESPOND BY . . .

Making it clear to them that you aren't choosing to succeed in some places and to struggle in others. You're doing the most you can with the talents you're lucky enough to have. And you are working hard to find ways to do better in areas where your talents aren't so strong.

SCHOOL SUCKS...
When You're Not Working Hard at All

WHILE NATURAL TALENT IS GENERALLY seen as positive, it can cut both ways. For every person with a gift for football or math, there's someone blessed with a talent for being distracted, uninterested, or another trait that makes it tough to achieve success. It's not that they lack the motivation; they're just saddled with certain challenges. And if anyone tries to light a fire under them, it leaves everyone frustrated and, well, burned. Fortunately, there are still ways to develop one's abilities to get the most out of school, no matter how naturally good you may be at being bad at it.

HERE'S AN EXAMPLE:
I wish that I could make my parents happy and do better

at school. But as much as they care, I really, honestly, truly don't. It all just seems kind of pointless and boring, and there are so many other things that I'd rather be doing with my time. My parents have tried everything to get me motivated, but at the end of the day, I just don't care. I don't like making my parents unhappy, but hey, I can live with it—school makes me pretty unhappy, too. So I guess we all have to live with some unhappiness until I'm done with school.

SIGNS YOU MAY BE MISINTERPRETING THINGS:

Maybe your lack of motivation isn't preventing you from learning as much as you think it is. You may be learning more than you realize. Or you're actually making decent use of your time, despite feeling indifferent or bored. It's possible you think you can't stand school and feel turned off by it because you're a perfectionist, haven't found a subject you love, or are more interested in non-school stuff.

. . . AND SIGNS YOU AREN'T:

You don't feel unmotivated about anything else in life— there's stuff you really love doing and look forward to. But teachers have told you and your parents that you're not applying yourself, so your lack of interest is easy to see, both from your demeanor and your report card. Perhaps you did make an effort once to look interested and got nothing out of it.

WHAT YOUR PARENTS SAY TO TRY TO HELP:

"School is important if you want to get a good job and make a decent living," or "If you gave school more effort, you'd feel better and people would respect you more."

. . . AND WHY IT ISN'T HELPFUL AT ALL:

The bored or unhappy feeling you get when you walk through the doors at school, and/or the lie-low-and-shut-up feeling you get in that particularly troublesome class, are hard to ignore. Parents may not remember or understand that, but being told you should be able to control those feelings and force yourself to be interested and happy just makes you feel even more frustrated.

WHAT YOU THINK YOU NEED TO FIGURE OUT IN ORDER TO FIX IT:

You hope to find a way to either feel even a little bit interested in school or never have to go to school again and get paid a *lot* of money to play video games.

WHY THOSE FIXES WILL FAIL:

You can't control a lot of your feelings about school. The strong feelings of boredom, sensitivity, and fear are part of your personality, and knowing what's bothering you won't make it change. And while dropping out might sound like a good solution—it isn't. Academics aside, getting through school teaches you necessary survival skills you can't learn anywhere else.

WHAT YOU CAN ACTUALLY DO ABOUT IT:

Once you accept the fact that you're a bit allergic to school (or just to certain elements of it), you don't need to keep looking for explanations or motivation. You can start thinking of better ways to learn, like through documentaries and independent reading, and focus on how to learn in your own way with the help of tutors or through hands-on experience with internships or volunteering. In the end, whether learning strikes you as fun or agony, it's always a survival skill. So your job is to avoid getting discouraged, distracted by self-pity, or derailed with trouble. You just need to get through it, period, without being distracted.

RED FLAGS TO LOOK FOR IN THE FUTURE:

Beware if you find yourself wanting to skip school to have fun instead. Particularly if you're falling in with a group of kids who do just that or are losing touch with the good kids you used to hang out with. Those are danger signs that your efforts to escape boredom are turning into bad habits that will make it harder for you to learn or to respect yourself.

THE UN-SUGARCOATED SUCKINESS YOU CAN EXPECT:

Unless you can make necessary changes, or until you can, every day is going to involve at least a small dose of suck. Expect boredom, frustration, and/or humiliation. Remember that school is not the ideal learning environment for everyone. But it's hard not to struggle with the feeling that you're failing, both in terms of grades and life, when good results are hard to come by.

THE UNTRUE SUCKINESS YOU MUST REJECT:

The idea that hating school will make you a failure forever, or that escaping from school and its responsibilities is the only way to be happy, is both a big fat lie and a massive waste of time. Just because school can't make you happy, and can make you very unhappy, doesn't mean that you can't find other ways and places to learn and grow. So keep looking for opportunities that might work for you. Thinking that happiness is an accurate indicator of something's worth is the biggest load of crap, because the most important things in life, from school to a career to marriage, require work. And work, by definition, is not always fun—even people who ski or hand model or eat pizza professionally sometimes just want a day off to nap, not shower, and watch *Golden Girls* reruns. And since work is a fundamental part of life, it's not something to try to avoid but something to start getting used to.

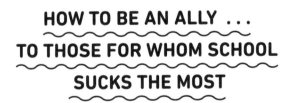

HOW TO BE AN ALLY . . .
TO THOSE FOR WHOM SCHOOL
SUCKS THE MOST

THE PROBLEM:

You promised your best friend that you'd help him with homework to get him through basketball season. But instead of helping him, you keep ending up doing his work for him.

WHAT YOU WANT TO DO:

Refuse to help him next time unless he actually wants help studying and not a homework servant.

. . . AND WHY YOU SHOULDN'T:

He'll feel hurt and defensive if you accuse him of using you. Because even if he is, he's probably not doing it on purpose. Plus, he's under so much pressure from his coach that your calling time might make him freak out.

WHAT YOU CAN DO:

Explain to him that you understand he's under a lot of stress. But unless he can find more time to put into the work, he won't have the confidence needed to put together his own answers on the exams and might still end up getting a bad grade. So you're going to give him as much of your time and effort as you can spare to make sure he can do the work and help him truly understand the material.

SCHOOL SUCKS . . .

When You're Working Hard
and It's Still the Worst

PRINCIPAL'S OFFICE

IN SO MANY WAYS, SCHOOL is just a small-scale version of life. It's often hard, unfair, and, for better or worse, it does come to an end. That's why, like in real life, hard work doesn't always pay off the way it should and good work isn't always given its proper reward. In both school and life, however, it's important not to let unfairness make you bitter, negative, and unable to find the point in pushing forward. Define your own reasons for working hard. The reasons don't have to depend on believing in the system or getting a positive reaction from others. If you take a stand for what's important to you, regardless of how it's received, you can learn to take anything crappy that life throws at you.

HERE'S AN EXAMPLE:

I'm not going to deny that I'm what most people would consider a nerd. I like most of my classes, but I do well even in the subjects I don't like because I'm just good at studying and staying focused. The downside is that being smart doesn't exactly make me popular (except when someone wants to "borrow" my answers). And since most kids treat me like I have the plague (or a permanent target on my back), it really doesn't make me happy. I know getting good grades is important, but if being a nerd feels this terrible, then maybe they aren't as important as everyone says.

SIGNS YOU MAY BE MISINTERPRETING THINGS:

It can be easy to pay more attention to negative reactions than to positive ones, especially when some of your classmates react with humiliation and/or violence. It's also easy to convince yourself that you're more miserable about the bad feedback than you are happy about your achievements. The same thing can happen if you need approval all the time or are just plain competitive.

. . . AND SIGNS YOU AREN'T:

The amount of bullying outweighs the number of compliments if you barely have time to enjoy an A before some jerk knocks his shoulder into you. You've thought about it and are sure that you can get along just fine in life without constant approval from others. It's really just the constant disapproval that's getting you down.

WHAT YOUR PARENTS SAY TO TRY TO HELP:

"Ignore what the other kids say; they're just jealous of your brains, so who cares?" or "You've got to ignore the turkeys and keep your eyes on the prize," or "You'll be the one laughing when you're a genius CEO and they're living in their parents' basement."

. . . AND WHY IT ISN'T HELPFUL AT ALL:

It's basically impossible to ignore what other people say when they're saying it constantly. Being told you should be able to feel better when you've tried really hard and actually can't, will always backfire. And having to hear that kind of thing over and over again discourages you from taking pride in your accomplishments and continuing to do what you do well. It's also hard to focus on possible future victories when your present is so crappy.

WHAT YOU THINK YOU NEED TO FIGURE OUT IN ORDER TO FIX IT:

You want to develop a thick, Vibranium-coated skin that will make you impervious to what other kids say or do. You also hope to find the trick for using your many skills to outsmart, impress, or conquer your tormentors.

WHY THOSE FIXES WILL FAIL:

It's not easy to control your reaction to criticism, and you can't ignore the hurt and loss of motivation when others constantly knock you down.

WHAT YOU CAN ACTUALLY DO ABOUT IT:

Even if you can't control how you feel about what others say and think, remember what you can get out of school. You are there to learn and to develop your interests, not to let social pressure or a drive for perfection turn you into someone you don't like. If your classmates can't appreciate/stop tormenting you, look for teachers to be mentors and allies. And look outside of school for nerds your age who share your outlook. Or just look for more activities outside of school, period, including classes at local community colleges.

RED FLAGS TO LOOK FOR IN THE FUTURE:

Beware of letting yourself spend time resenting the unfairness of how you're being mistreated rather than spending time doing constructive things that make you strong. Avoid indulging in too much complaining or hanging out with complainers, because dwelling on anger and mistreatment will make you feel like a helpless victim and push you to do less, give up, or act out.

THE UN-SUGARCOATED SUCKINESS YOU CAN EXPECT:

Your talent or your perceived lack of coolness will continue to cause you to feel frustration, sadness, and general crappiness. And it will also tempt you to fight back, either by trying to do more or to do less.

THE UNTRUE SUCKINESS YOU MUST REJECT:

Don't let the pain of unfair bullying slow you down or drive you to try harder to seek your bullies' approval. If you're doing your best at getting the most out of school, then you know you will eventually grow stronger and more independent. Just because your gets are being rewarded with punishment doesn't mean that there's no point in trying or that your accomplishments are worthless. If anything, the opposite is true; if you can achieve your goals despite being surrounded by discouragement and injustice, then your actions have that much more meaning and value. Don't hesitate to seek help from a supportive adult, even a counselor, if you need it. Getting through school, or life in general, without giving up on your goals or yourself, despite getting crapped on every day, is far more important than what people think of all the As you get.

SCHOOL SUCKS: THE POINT

Many people see school as a land full of opportunities that rewards the diligent and hardworking. But unfortunately, sometimes that's not the case. Uncontrollable, undeserved bad luck may interfere with your ability to succeed, regardless of how much effort you make and how many chances you're given. So think of trying hard as the best method for finding out what works and what doesn't, not as a sure path to success. Then, if you get hit with some bad luck and your good efforts end up getting you nowhere, don't fall into the trap of getting down on yourself or deciding that learning isn't worthwhile. Instead, give yourself credit for making use of your strengths while figuring out how to manage your weaknesses. Yes, you may have to work harder than you would like to, and your results may not reflect those efforts or fulfill others' expectations. But you're always on the right track when you're doing your best to learn new things and develop your abilities, no matter how

slowly it goes or how you compare to others along the way. When you continue to learn, in spite of poor grades, critical comments, and other obstacles, you're earning extra credit in the "life sucks" class.

CHAPTER THREE

CULTURAL DIFFERENCES SUCK

WHEN THE COLOR OF YOUR skin, the accent of your speech, or the literal nose on your face isn't like everyone else's, it can make you feel different, isolated, frustrated, or trapped. When you can't change yourself in order to fit in, and you can't change other people's minds, it's easy to feel miserable, at least some of the time. And it's easy to think that fitting in is something you could learn how to do, if you could find the right way to dress and walk and talk or find a competent plastic surgeon.

Dealing with ignorance and discrimination is hard for anyone, no matter their age. But when you're in school, which can feel like a daily trial in front of a nasty jury of your peers, the burden is especially heavy. It's almost impossible not to envy kids who are in the cultural majority, and it might make you blame your pain on your own heritage and culture. You may doubt yourself, value what you aren't, hate what you are, and reject what your parents and family have taught you to believe in.

Some adults might say that cultural differences can be overcome if you just have pride in yourself, are understanding, and replace hate and suspicion with kindness and love. Unfortunately, their well-intended advice can make your self-rejection worse if it encourages you to expect the impossible.

Of course, reaching out and getting to know people who are different from you is a worthwhile goal. Differences in color, culture, and religion can make friendships more interesting. They can also open your mind to the many differences that exist in our country and the world. But when cultural differences among you, your classmates, and your parents make you feel frustrated and isolated, you need to know when you can improve things and when you can't.

That doesn't mean giving up hope. Even when there's no way to bridge the cultural differences that separate you from other people in your life, remember that you're never as helpless or alone as you feel. You will become better able to protect yourself from prejudice as you grow up and learn to value what you know about yourself, your ethnicity, faith, culture, and all the aspects of you that make you—well, you.

But it won't be easy, and it's hard when you have classmates who seem to fit in all the time, who don't have to question their customs and beliefs, and who don't seem to have a moment of suffering in their perfect lives. Remember, however, that by not having to question who they are, those classmates miss the opportunity to discover what they value most about themselves, where they come from, and how they wish to shape who they are going to become.

So don't feel responsible for changing the unchangeable to ease the pain of feeling, and being, different. Learn to tolerate that pain while growing to appreciate the ways your culture or ethnicity make you different. Eventually, you will come to compare your customs and values to the majority's based on your own experience, not the nasty put-downs of other kids, and decide which traditions work best for you.

You may never fit in easily with certain classmates or people in your neighborhood. But, if you can tolerate that alienation without tearing yourself down or learning to hate others, you will work out what you do and don't have in common and what you can and can't share. And, regardless of differences, you will have an easier time being comfortable with yourself and with people you meet now and for the rest of your life.

HOW TO BALANCE CAUTION WITH COURAGE FOR CULTURAL UNDERSTANDING:

Getting to know people from other cultures can be very rewarding, but it requires a willingness to learn new rules and customs as well as the courage to take chances and expose yourself to the unknown. Without that courage, your life experience will be narrow, and without the willingness to learn, you may say or do things that offend the people you're trying to connect with. So it's important to develop a level of awareness that prepares you to deal with problems while also welcoming new experiences. Cultural outreach won't reward you with a degree, trophy, or slain dragon, but it will make you a smarter, better person, and at the very least, it will make you some good friends. Here is a quiz to help you figure out where you stand.

1 A few days after your friend's grandmother dies, you're invited to his house for an event to mourn her death. **Even though you know nothing about his religion, you want to be there for him, so you:**

A) Read up a little on what this tradition is about so you know what to wear and how to act. This way, you'll be there for your friend without offending his entire family during a particularly sad time.

B) Decide to play it cool and go over as if it were just a normal hangout, since you don't really know what his tradition is.

C) Send him a nice email, but that's it. You don't feel comfortable participating in a religious event you don't know anything about.

2 While your old school was really diverse, the one in your new town really, really isn't. Which means you're now one of the few people of color there. Your immediate reaction is to:

A) Be nervous, because you don't know what the situation will be like or how your classmates will react to you. But you are also determined to keep your head up, make friends, avoid enemies, and get the most out of your new school.

B) Figure it probably doesn't make a difference—it certainly won't to you—so you'll just go in, be your friendly self, and it should go great.

C) Freak out and beg your parents to spare you from going to a school where you'll surely be teased, ostracized, or bullied.

3 Your girlfriend says she's no longer okay with keeping your relationship secret. But you're certain that you'll never be able to see her, or possibly daylight, again if your family finds out that you're dating someone from outside your community. You don't want to lose her, so you decide to:

A) Tell her that, as much as you care about her, there's no way for the two of you to go public without making your life hell and ruining your relationship, at least until you figure out a way to even approach the topic with your parents. So if she can't see the wisdom of keeping your relationship private for now, you don't see any choice but to break up, even though you really don't want to stop seeing her or cause her pain.

B) Do what it takes to keep seeing her—even if it means lying to her about your family's approval—hoping that, by some miracle, if they do find out, they will withhold their wrath and grow to like her. **C)** Tell her no way. As much as you want to stay together, you realize it was a mistake to ever go against your parents' wishes and date her in the first place. You'll miss her, and your freedom, when you voluntarily flee to a monastery (or its equivalent) to properly repent.

IF YOUR ANSWERS WERE MAINLY As:

Your balance is just right. You're sensitive to cultural differences. You realize that people can be offended for reasons you don't understand and can't predict, so you're careful to be polite and respectful. You also know that, despite your efforts, those differences may still make you the target of criticism or bullying. So you try not to overreact, take things personally, or generally let issues of cultural identity get in your way while getting to know people who are culturally different and being your best self.

IF YOUR ANSWERS WERE MAINLY Bs:

You need to be more cautious, careful, and observant. You're tolerant and accepting of differences, which is good. But your tolerance is due mostly to pretending they aren't there, which isn't so great. Those differences can put you or your friends in danger or cause unintended pain, so recognizing and being prepared for them is necessary for your safety. Instead of assuming that everyone is just like you and that things will always be okay, learn to recognize differences and avoid misunderstandings that might cause pain or conflict.

IF YOUR ANSWERS WERE MAINLY Cs:

You're too frightened of differences and assume that trouble is inevitable. Spending time with people who aren't like you makes you so uncomfortable that you're sure it will turn out badly. So you act tough, get ready to run, and avoid people who are different, which makes things turn out badly and confirms your fears. Instead, challenge your fears by getting to know some people who are different from you. Your goal isn't to get along with everyone but to learn the value of personal and cultural differences while making constructive use of your fear to identify real problems.

DO MY PARENTS HAVE A POINT?
• • • • • • • • • • • • • • • • • • •

WHEN YOUR PARENTS SAY . . .

"Have all the crushes you want, but you can only date or be friends with people who are the same religion/color/ethnicity as us if you want our approval."

IT SOUNDS DUMB BECAUSE . . .

You believe there are more important things than religion, color, and ethnicity when it comes to friendship and dating. And basing their approval and respect on those factors alone isn't just unfair, it's closed-minded and unreasonable.

BUT IT'S NOT DUMB TO THEM BECAUSE . . .

Their rules may have less to do with their dislike or distrust of people who aren't like them and more to do with their fear of your losing your cultural or religious identity. Which, again, is something they see as valuable, in their own lives and as a tie to yours.

SO BE SMART AND . . .

Don't call them bigoted or closed-minded. While it may accurately describe their position, it will hurt them and may cause them to find fault with your decisions and morals.

THEN RESPOND BY . . .

Telling them that their respect and approval mean the world to you. But you think it's also important to choose friends who are kind, thoughtful, and loyal, regardless of their color, nationality, or faith. And you hope they'll learn to trust your ability to find good friends, both inside and outside your culture. In the meantime, you'll avoid openly disrespecting their rules while reserving your right to be kind to anyone who deserves it.

CULTURAL DIFFERENCES SUCK . . .

When You Feel Alienated
from the Culture at Home

THE MORE RIGID YOUR PARENTS are about their beliefs, the more likely you are to come into conflict with them as you get older. When you were little and less independent, you didn't notice the rules or they may not have affected you as much. But now that you're older, you may discover that your cultural and religious values differ from your parents' in ways that they may not be able to accept. They may see their culture and traditions as essential to your becoming a good adult and to protecting you from danger and evil. Your instincts may tell you to win their understanding, change their minds, or show them that they can't control you, and retaliate. Which just proves to them that you need more guidance, control, rules, and perhaps more punishment. So instead of dismissing, rebelling against, or repeatedly trying to win over your parents, pursue the goals you started out with: to quietly find your own values and rules, to get equipped for adulthood, and to accept your parents, even if it's hard for them to accept you. As hard as it may be to do, focus on finding what's right for you, not proving your parents wrong.

HERE'S AN EXAMPLE:

I know my parents love me. And I wish they knew that I still love them even though I don't agree with their ideas about how I'm supposed to behave. They're extremely religious and believe that girls should be modest and keep their opinions to themselves, particularly when they're in the company of men. It was easy to follow that when I was little, but now that I'm older it doesn't make sense to me. I don't want to defer to my brothers, and I know how to dress appropriately. I just can't see myself following their rules, but I also can't see how I can get them to understand.

SIGNS YOU MAY BE MISINTERPRETING THINGS:

Your parents have given you no reason to believe they

don't genuinely love you and want you to be happy. So you may be overestimating how upset they'll be if you openly disagree with some of their beliefs. And maybe you're being unfair by assuming they'll react to any dissent with anger and rejection.

. . . AND SIGNS YOU AREN'T:

Based on how you've seen them react to "inappropriate" behavior or talk in the past, you know that, when it comes to judgment, your parents don't hold back. They've made it very clear that they take their beliefs very seriously, hold other parents responsible for how their kids behave, and are very critical of anyone who falls even a hair short of their standards.

WHAT YOUR PARENTS SAY TO TRY TO HELP:

"If you don't honor your religious heritage then you won't be able to respect yourself, and nobody else will respect you, either," or "Everyone has doubts at your age, but time and experience will only strengthen your faith," or "It's not our place to question the traditions of our faith."

. . . AND WHY IT ISN'T HELPFUL AT ALL:

They believe that being a good person requires you to

conform completely with their customs and beliefs, but you've come to disagree with that. So the more they urge you to live within their rules, the more they push you away. But you can't force your doubts to go away. Plus, it's not that you're questioning all religious beliefs, just the strict way your parents choose to interpret them.

WHAT YOU THINK YOU NEED TO FIGURE OUT IN ORDER TO FIX IT:

You wish you could find the right words to assure your parents that you love them and value their religious teachings about right and wrong, and that they have nothing to fear from your adopting certain ideas or customs that are different from theirs. You would like them to believe that you will turn out all right, even if you don't share all their beliefs or wish to continue all their customs.

WHY THOSE FIXES WILL FAIL:

No matter what good words they hear from you, your parents can't stop being afraid of what will happen if you stray from the customs and rules of your culture. That's because parents can't stop being afraid for their children, period. They worry about all the dangers and bad luck that life can throw at you. And a life experience very different from yours has taught them to rely on traditions and beliefs that they feel obliged to preserve. So pushing hard to change the way your parents think by wearing them down, challenging their rules, or urging them to see how what you're doing isn't wrong is likely to backfire. It's actually more likely that you'll rob yourself of time and energy needed for more important things and take the focus off your goal of learning, growing, and becoming independent.

WHAT YOU CAN ACTUALLY DO ABOUT IT:

Just as you shouldn't feel bad for forming your own judgments about your parents' rules, customs, and religion, you also shouldn't expect to feel good when they try to set you straight and refuse to hear your side. Instead, treat them with your usual respect while biting your tongue, finding more sympathetic adults or peers to talk to, and continuing to look for whatever is worthwhile in their rituals and values. Just because you don't agree with their overall take on their religious practices doesn't mean that certain elements may not be worthwhile. So ask yourself whether there are any of your family's religious rituals or values that do help you to focus or find perspective, or show you the right things to do. If all this sounds like work, you're right. In the end, expect to find beliefs and rules that work for you, to credit your parents for helping you get there, and to accept that there may be certain cultural and religious differences, like beliefs about gender equality, that are perhaps better not talked about.

RED FLAGS TO LOOK FOR IN THE FUTURE:

Since your goal is to keep your cultural or religious differences from starting a civil war between you and your parents, try not to lose your temper, waste energy on trying to change them or win their approval, or talk, dress, or act in ways that offend them and that they will definitely condemn you for. If you're doing more to prove your parents wrong or show them that you've been treated unfairly than you are to do well at school and be a good friend—i.e., be a good person—then you're heading for heartache (but not necessarily, say, damnation).

THE UN-SUGARCOATED SUCKINESS YOU CAN EXPECT:

You may not be able to escape constant supervision, control, and frequent unfair criticism. If that's the case, you will find yourself feeling unhappy, angry, and helpless.

(And of course, if those feelings motivate you to openly rebel or attempt to change your parents' minds, things will get even worse.) Even if you are allowed to explore your own ideas and beliefs, continuing to go through the religious motions with your parents may frustrate you and make you feel like you're surrendering to values you don't like or believe in. Sucking it up will suck, but have faith in your ability to privately disagree with your parents without becoming the bad person they most fear you will become and whom you really don't want to be.

THE UNTRUE SUCKINESS YOU MUST REJECT:

Your parents want the best for you, but it's up to you to determine what it means to be a good person. It's important to stand up to your parents about your own beliefs and ideas, but it's just as, or even more, important to get well equipped for life and grow into a decent person. So instead of killing them with conflict, be a living example of how you can still be good. You can accomplish important goals and live up to shared values, even if you don't follow all their ideas. The key is finding your own values and place in the world without putting it in your parents' faces.

HOW TO BE AN ALLY . . .
TO SOMEONE WHO ISN'T A MEMBER OF THE
CULTURAL/ETHNIC MAJORITY

THE PROBLEM:

Some people in your class are giving a new kid a hard time because he has a strong foreign accent.

WHAT YOU WANT TO DO:

Call them out for being jerks and get them to back off.

. . . AND WHY YOU SHOULDN'T:

It could just make things hard for you and worse for him. Plus, you don't really know this kid, and he might resent the extra attention your taking a stand would bring.

WHAT YOU CAN DO:

Find a time when the jerks aren't around and talk to this kid and try to get to know him. If it seems like he could be a friend, introduce him to your other friends since there's always strength in numbers. If it doesn't, you can at least tell him you're sorry these kids are being jerks and offer him suggestions for avoiding them and finding adult support.

CULTURAL DIFFERENCES SUCK . . .

When Your Culture Makes You Feel Alienated at School

WE'VE BEEN TOLD NOT TO judge a book by its cover, but at a certain point in life, most people start to use their cover—that is, the way they dress, the way they wear their hair, whatever—to tell the world their story. And that's all fine and good if your book is like all the other ones in the library, but not if your cover is dominated or defined by a religion or culture that makes you stand out. Then, all the other signals you're trying to send with your sneaker game or lip color may be drowned out by the head covering, clothing, or jewelry that are part of your cultural identity and that the people around you can't seem to get past. Instead of fighting to fit in and becoming endlessly and needlessly frustrated and self-critical, learn to value what you stand for, despite its not being easy or popular. If you can embrace who you are, then you won't miss the friendship or approval of those who can't be bothered to crack your cover and read your pages. And you won't miss the boat when you finally come across people with the "reading skills" to be your real friends.

HERE'S AN EXAMPLE:

I get along well with my parents. I'm a lot less observant than they are and we disagree about a lot of stuff, but I choose to wear hijab and am proud to be Muslim. However, being so obviously Muslim in a mostly Christian town and school isn't helping me make friends. I think a lot of my classmates avoid me because they think I'm really religious and conservative, like I'll tell on them for even swearing in my presence. I just want to make friends, and I hate feeling like I'm strange because I wear a head scarf.

SIGNS YOU MAY BE MISINTERPRETING THINGS:

Though some kids may say nasty things about you behind your back, there may be more kids who are open-minded about cultural differences and are possible friends. If you're naturally shy, and that shyness is stopping you from putting yourself out there and actively trying to make friends, then other kids may be mistaking your shyness for unfriendliness.

. . . AND SIGNS YOU AREN'T:

You've never thought of yourself as particularly shy. In fact, you've made a real effort to meet people by getting involved in extracurriculars, attending school events, or just being as friendly as possible in the hallways and when you're assigned to group projects in class. But, despite your best efforts, no one sits next to you at lunch, invites you to hang out, or is anything more than distantly friendly.

WHAT YOUR PARENTS SAY TO TRY TO HELP:

"Those kids are acting that way because they're actually jealous of how smart and well mannered you are," or "Kids here are all disrespectful and badly behaved, so we're glad you don't have much to do with them," or "Nobody will care what you look or sound like if you make it clear to everyone that you're polite, friendly, and eager to fit in."

. . . AND WHY IT ISN'T HELPFUL AT ALL:

Chalking up the problem to the other kids being jealous or prejudiced just reminds you that your parents sometimes sound pretty prejudiced themselves. Especially when they assume that you're the only not-horrible kid in your class (or the world). And you would hope your parents would trust you to avoid befriending jerks. Finally, you've already tried being nice and friendly and it hasn't worked, so your parents suggesting that it should work just makes you feel like you're not doing it right, which is neither true nor fair.

WHAT YOU THINK YOU NEED TO FIGURE OUT IN ORDER TO FIX IT:

You're sure that if you could just make friends with one person, that would break the curse and people would start to see you as a normal, friend-able human being. Or maybe kids would stop being so standoffish if you could just educate them about your culture. A longer shot would be finding a surefire way to win the admiration of your classmates—maybe through acquiring some previously unknown skill or becoming Internet famous—so that your difference wouldn't matter anymore.

WHY THOSE FIXES WILL FAIL:

Even if making just one friend would turn the tide— and there's no guarantee that it would—getting anyone to take a chance and break away from the herd is a tall order. After all, as someone familiar with the pain of being shunned, you understand why others would be hesitant to risk it.

WHAT YOU CAN ACTUALLY DO ABOUT IT:

As we said before, school is like a job. In this situation, if all your friendship efforts have failed, accepting the limits of friendship and social approval makes it necessary to create "work relationships" at school. Unlike a friendship, a work relationship is based less on sharing personal feelings or secrets and more on just sharing physical space in a polite, positive atmosphere. So find ways to work together respectfully and productively without getting too personal. Keep a "professional" distance and actively but politely pursue your interests. And as soon as those interests give you an opportunity to work with people, whether it's on homework or sports, show them that you're friendly-but-not-personal, have good ideas, and are eager to do your share. Then, when they start to relax a bit, some may begin to open up and allow for real friendships to occur. Your goal, however, isn't to force anyone to be friends. It's to learn how to do what's important, remain friendly, and avoid bitterness, despite feeling lonely and friendless. And then to respect yourself for handling a tough job like a pro.

RED FLAGS TO LOOK FOR IN THE FUTURE:

Avoid letting your disappointment and isolation get the best of you. And try not to react to classmates who are provocative jerks by being a jerk yourself. If you respond by meeting their insults with insults, you'll just give more power to their nastiness and reinforce all the stereotypes they believe in. If you need to stand up for yourself, never sink to their level. Also, don't let loneliness push you into relationships with people who aren't really solid and reliable.

THE UN-SUGARCOATED SUCKINESS YOU CAN EXPECT:

Switching your goal from making friends to making the best of things can stop the self-blame, but it can't always protect you from feeling lonely, rejected, and helpless. You may also have to deal with unhelpful comments made worse by your parents' attempts to help with well-intentioned advice.

THE UNTRUE SUCKINESS YOU MUST REJECT:

It can be excruciating to feel disconnected from or

rejected by the people you're stuck spending hours with every day. And the lack of a good solution makes it even more painful. But as tough as it may be, keep doing "your work" and hold your head high. Be polite and decent, even when you're feeling that no one wants to talk to you. The strength you're gaining by surviving and learning from this experience will be invaluable in the future, not just with making friends and dealing with work, but with anything life throws your way.

Remember: Put Common Decency Above Culture

We're often taught to be kind to and accepting of people from all cultures. That's certainly a goal worth working toward, but being open and friendly toward everyone is often difficult, even those from your own culture and especially if they rub you the wrong way. The real lesson, then, is to behave decently toward others. This won't always be easy, and it may not always be possible, but it's the best way to approach the situation.

Yes, we should always give everyone a chance and try to put aside our prejudices, get to know them, and understand how things look from their point of view. But as hard as we may try to be tolerant and compassionate of others, the way we ultimately feel about them and how much we like or dislike them are often out of our control, no matter what we do. So feeling like you're supposed to like someone you can't, whether they're from an unfamiliar background and culture or not, is a sure way to stir up more negativity than you started with.

But even if someone is from a culture you have an unshakable prejudice toward, you don't have to have a kumbaya moment in order to treat them with respect. You don't have to learn to love that culture in order to see someone as an individual human being who deserves the same respect as anyone else. Having good feelings toward all people is an admirable achievement that may make the world a better place, but it isn't going to happen anytime soon. On the other hand, learning to be respectful and positive toward people you don't like is a greater achievement that will make you a better person.

CULTURAL DIFFERENCES SUCK...
When You Don't Fit In with the Culture at School or at Home

EVEN IF YOU DON'T SHARE your parents' cultural beliefs, you still share the same experience of living within that culture. If you're living in a place where you're outsiders, at least you're outsiders together. Once your experience starts to diverge, however—as it must when you grow up in a new culture that isn't theirs and are exposed to new ideas and opportunities—a rift may begin to grow. On the plus side, you may have chances to learn and get ahead that other members of your family may not have had.

The negative side, however, is that you'll likely end up feeling like you don't completely fit in anywhere. Instead of letting the sense of alienation sap your confidence, learn to appreciate your unique perspective as you forge your own path.

HERE'S AN EXAMPLE:

I'm on track to be the first person in my family to go to college. My parents are proud of me, but some people in my family don't feel that way. They accuse me of thinking I'm too good for them, or that I don't need them anymore. I try to explain that I'm not ignoring them. I'm just busy (with a ton of homework, afterschool activities, my work-study job . . . it never ends), but they think I'm making excuses, so I can't win. And my classmates don't really understand my situation because I come from a world that is so different from theirs. I'm living in two worlds but I don't fit into either, and I wish I could figure out where I belong.

SIGNS YOU MAY BE MISINTERPRETING THINGS:

Even if your relatives don't seem to get exactly what you're going through, that doesn't mean they're so oblivious that they don't care or can't offer some sort of valuable support. You could also be finding it hard to make friends with classmates because you've tried too hard to fit in with a group you think you're supposed to belong to, rather than looking for individuals who might be friends.

. . . AND SIGNS YOU AREN'T:

The criticism from your family doesn't stop. You've tried making friends with individuals as well as groups, but there's always that moment when your "otherness" becomes clear. And it leaves you feeling humiliated and lonelier than if you were just by yourself.

WHAT YOUR PARENTS SAY TO TRY TO HELP:

"If you respect your heritage and don't try to put on airs, you'll find other kids will respect you for who you are," or "Just tell those kids that it's who you are, not where you come from, that matters."

. . . AND WHY IT ISN'T HELPFUL AT ALL:

Their advice implies that you can find acceptance, at school and at home, if you do the right thing, when it's often just not possible. You're also not sure if you've won the respect of your classmates, but you are sure that none of that respect has translated into what you really care about—actual friendship. And your parents' lack of understanding makes you feel distanced from them, as well. What you're trying to tell them is that your problem is the lack of another person like you to be friends with.

WHAT YOU THINK YOU NEED TO FIGURE OUT IN ORDER TO FIX IT:

You wish you had the ability to find a classmate who would be interested in learning about where you came from, rather than just vaguely accepting you because you're nice, which could then perhaps start a trend. Then you might actually be able to relate and get to know each other. And you wish you were confident enough so that you didn't need support from your parents or care what they thought about your troubles, so you didn't wind up resenting their inability to understand when you know they're trying hard to help.

WHY THOSE FIXES WILL FAIL:

Since mass interest in understanding your culture seems about as likely as checkers becoming trendy, you know it's unrealistic to pin your hopes on that. Ultimately, you can't change the way you or others feel about your culture, the way you need your parents' support, or the way they assume they know you, no matter how hard you try to communicate otherwise.

WHAT YOU CAN ACTUALLY DO ABOUT IT:

Through no fault of your own, fitting in is often

impossible. So your job is to be decent to other people and to get your work done in spite of the emotional pain. It may help to think of yourself less as someone struggling to fit in and more as a scientist observing a group of unknown creatures. You live among them, but at a safe distance. Also, keep an eye out for fellow outsiders, even if they're not outsiders in the same way you are. Focus on the things you have in common, instead of the obvious things you don't. You may currently feel like it's you against the world, but if you can get the most out of your current situation, you'll eventually gain access to new opportunities.

RED FLAGS TO LOOK FOR IN THE FUTURE:

Loneliness can be hard, but falling in with crappy friends creates greater problems. Don't lower your friendship standards so you can have any friends, period. And don't become bitter, deciding that those at school who act indifferent to you actually hate you and therefore deserve your scorn. Isolation can undermine motivation, so don't let solitude stop you from respecting yourself and moving forward.

THE UN-SUGARCOATED SUCKINESS YOU CAN EXPECT:

You can't help feeling stuck between two worlds that

don't understand or accept you as much as you need. Your family, regardless of how much they love you, may not be able to understand your problem, accept your differences, or make you feel comforted and successful.

THE UNTRUE SUCKINESS YOU MUST REJECT:

Just because there are many ways that being different can make life suck and create a gap between you, your schoolmates, and your parents, being different does not inherently suck or mean that you suck, period. The culture your family comes from is always going to be a part of you. You don't have to love it and be proud of it all the time, and it may sometimes cause you pain, but you can always learn from it, find something good in it, and make something better from it in the future. Begin by accepting it, along with the fact that life is often hard and unfair and that your peers at times may act like ignorant jerks. If you can't make it happen, don't make yourself responsible for winning over the jerks, gaining the recognition you feel you deserve for who you are, or finding a way to be happier with your parents. Don't waste time looking for ways to solve the problems that aren't going away. Instead, aim to manage them by avoiding unnecessary conflict, going with the flow, and reminding yourself that the pain you're dealing with now is the price for a better future.

CULTURAL DIFFERENCES SUCK: THE POINT

If everyone you knew came from the same place, followed the same religion, and looked the same, it would, of course, be easier to avoid cultural bias and misunderstanding. Everyone would be happier. On the other hand, it would be harder to find opportunities to grow, explore new ideas, and gain new perspectives. So if you're hurt by the non-acceptance that goes with these differences, whether at home or at school, don't feel you have to suppress those differences or change yourself in

order to feel more comfortable. Instead, ask yourself what you value most in the culture you come from, the ones you encounter, and the one you wish to create and pass on. If you accept and learn from these differences, you'll build a circle of friends who also value strength of character above all, which is one of the best traits to share with anyone.

CHAPTER FOUR

BODIES SUCK

BODIES CAN BE PROBLEMATIC, ESPECIALLY since your body affects the way you eat, learn, move, talk, and behave. But despite new medical advances, diets, health apps, and so on, issues with your health and appearance can never be completely avoided nor made to disappear.

A lot of health issues are never cured, only managed, and not being able to get better is frustrating. After all, being healthy would mean being normal, which would seemingly make everything better. In reality, not only is being healthy or "normal" rarely in our control, it also doesn't guarantee a happy life. Nor does being beautiful guarantee a great one, especially if your beauty attracts people who are obsessed with looks over character.

In fact, ideas about bodies, be they less or more than ideal, have the power to infect and distort our behavior and our character, but only if we let them. Body- and health-inspired insecurity and negativity will tell us to reject and shame whatever disgusts us, including ourselves. They can also make us blame the sick or different-looking person for being or looking "wrong" as well as irrationally fear that we may "catch" those differences ourselves.

Your goal, then, isn't to make yourself more healthy and beautiful than is possible or persuade yourself and other people to overlook your physical flaws or illness. Instead, it's to learn how to realistically define beauty, both overall and for yourself. This way you can manage your desire for beauty and avoid the ugliness that the need for beauty can create. And if other people direct that ugliness at you because of your body, your job is to protect yourself from their behavior. That will help you grow stronger and better as a person, even if you encounter illness and imperfections, unkind people, and negative feelings about bodies that may never completely go away.

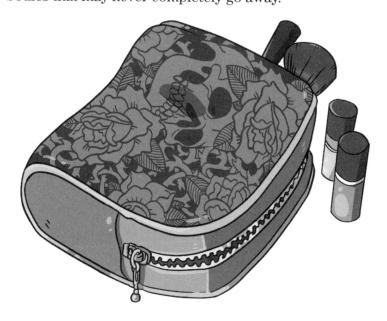

Having poor health, an atypical appearance, or a disability will create difficulties for you that many people may never have to experience. But experiencing and accepting those difficulties can also help you to develop an amazing ability to be strong, decent, and immune to the damaging effects that being different often causes.

HOW TO DETERMINE YOUR OWN SMART STANDARDS FOR HEALTH AND APPEARANCE

Sensible definitions of health and beauty, like health and beauty themselves, are more than skin-deep. Valuing your gym time and designer labels doesn't necessarily make you evil and superficial. And walking around all day oblivious to the toothpaste on your face doesn't mean you don't care about your appearance

Ultimately, it's not just about how much perfect health and beauty mean to you. It's about whether you prioritize unattainable attractiveness and health over more important values, such as friendship, hard work, and being a good person. Here's a quiz to help you figure out where you fall.

1 The shoes that everyone must have cost so much that you'll only be able to get a pair yourself if you put in extra hours at your part-time job (or pull off a bank heist). You decide to:

A) Determine whether you have the time to even try to get that kind of money, and if you don't, try to figure out whether there are cheaper shoes out there that may get you a decent rating on the cool scale.

B) Flip burgers, beg, or sell everything you own to get a pair, because you cannot be seen in anything but the best.

C) Be content with the shoes you already have that your mom got you last year, because you don't really care about shoes, anyway.

2 While you usually stay pretty active, an injury grounded you for a few months, making it impossible for you to comfortably do anything but sit on the couch. As a result, you've put on a bunch of pounds. Now that you're back on your feet, your first instinct is to:

A) Leave the house, see friends, and generally enjoy your freedom and ability to be active again. Your hope is that returning to your normal life will also get you back to your normal weight. But if it doesn't, you'll talk to your doctor about ways you can change your diet and add some exercise to get back on track.

B) Start running every day until you lose every last, blessed pound.

C) Ask your mom to pick up some sweatpants for you and just put those on until the weight goes away (or doesn't, whatever).

3 One of your good friends was in a bad car accident that left her with a pretty intense scar on her upper arm. And that's made her self-conscious about wearing T-shirts, even in really hot weather. When she mutters something about

how uncomfortable she is in the heat, you tell her to:

A) Just put on a tank top, because, yes, people might stare, but then that's their problem. And if anyone does stare, you'll tell them she got the scar when she was attacked by a shark and won. So unless they think they're tougher than a shark, they'd better back off.

B) Let you know what you can do to help, because you'll do whatever it takes to hide the scar. Especially because it's embarrassing to be seen with her when she's all sweaty.

C) Explain to you why she doesn't just wear something more lightweight, because you never realized she had a scar in the first place. In fact, you wouldn't notice if she wore wool sweaters all summer long because you're essentially blind to fashion.

4 **One of your close friends had to go to the hospital for a few weeks because she got really depressed and hurt herself. You haven't been able to visit, but when she gets out tomorrow, you're going to:**

A) See her at home to check on how she's doing and make sure she knows you're there for her and ready to talk about what happened when she is.

B) Text her to see if she's okay, then go back to being nice but keep your distance. Because you'd rather not be seen with her until you can feel confident that this was a one-time thing that won't happen again and not a sign that your friend is kind of broken.

C) Get in touch like nothing happened, then continue acting like nothing happened. Because what happened is none of your business, you don't know the right thing to say, anyway, and she's probably all better now, so there's no reason to make it into a big deal.

ANSWER KEY

IF YOUR ANSWERS WERE MAINLY As:

Your standards are realistic and reasonable. You like to look and feel good but not to the point where these goals control you. You know how people react to the way you look or feel, but you don't let your desire for positive feedback interfere with the things that you consider more important, like being a good friend, getting your work done, and generally being a good person. Your standards are fair, at least in terms of how you judge both yourself and others.

IF YOUR ANSWERS WERE MAINLY Bs:

Your expectations are way too high. You're not only conscious of, but maybe a bit obsessed with appearance. You've got lots of determination and discipline, and you're ready to work hard to meet your high standards and win the admiration of others. Unfortunately, you forget your health, your friendships, and other important priorities and values in the process. Looking good should never take priority over being a good person, even if doing the right thing isn't always pretty.

IF YOUR ANSWERS WERE MAINLY Cs:

Your expectations are too low. There's something admirable about how totally oblivious you are to appearance and to the ways people respond to you. On the other hand, this can sometimes come off as being too insensitive to others. People can misinterpret your inability to notice certain things as purposefully ignoring stuff they care about, which can leave them feeling hurt and offended.

DO MY FRIENDS HAVE A POINT?

WHEN YOUR FRIEND SAYS . . .

"Don't say that you look fat—you look beautiful!"

IT SOUNDS DUMB BECAUSE . . .

Being fat isn't ugly, so you can be fat and beautiful at the same time.

But even if you called yourself fat because you do think you look ugly, it might be hard to think your friend is being honest and not just being nice.

BUT IT'S NOT DUMB TO YOUR FRIEND BECAUSE . . .

Like too many people—possibly yourself included—your friend seems to think that being fat is unattractive. And since your friend loves you, she doesn't like to hear you be mean to yourself. And she is probably being honest because people who love you always see the beauty in you, even when you can't.

SO BE SMART AND . . .

Stop giving voice to your inner enemy. Doing that just gives those negative thoughts power. Before you say and legitimize something self-critical in front of your friends, be your own friend, defend yourself from your own mean comments, and shut them down before they get a chance to be said out loud. Acknowledge that being whatever weight you are doesn't make you ugly. If your weight is bothering you, you can talk to your doctor about healthy ways to address it, but your first priority should be to stop believing in the stigma attached to size.

THEN RESPOND BY . . .

Thinking through your own intentions. If you were calling yourself fat to put yourself down, thank her for being a good friend. Tell her that you'll try to stop yourself from being so negative in the future. If you were just making a factual statement about your size, explain that you appreciate what she's trying to do, but you weren't trying to put yourself down. Let her know that you don't think there's anything wrong with your size, so neither should she.

BODIES SUCK . . .
When You're Sick

NO MATTER HOW HEALTHY YOU eat, how much exercise you get, or how good your genes are, you're still vulnerable to illness and its power to mess with your body and your life. It's easy to feel like a failure when you can't control your health or even your symptoms. In truth, the only thing you've failed to do is have great luck. Your strength as a person is never defined by your health. It's defined by your ability to pursue the things that matter most as best you can, despite the effects of a persistent illness on your ability to perform everyday tasks.

HERE'S AN EXAMPLE:

I've had really bad allergies my whole life. I've grown out of some of them, but the ones I still have are so severe that I really wonder why my parents don't just take me out of school and put me on a space station. The school gave me a special table at lunch, but then this group of jerks threw peanuts at me, so now I have to eat in an empty classroom. I can't play sports because I could end up having an asthma attack so severe that they'd have to call an ambulance. The kids who aren't jerks are too afraid to hang out with me because they think just hanging out at someone's house might kill me. No one hates me, but people work so hard to avoid me that my joke is that they seem allergic to *me* . . . except it's not funny and I really hate it.

SIGNS YOU MAY BE MISINTERPRETING THINGS:

Your self-consciousness may be driving you to avoid people. And while that can protect you from stares and teasing, it can also make it hard for anyone who's sincerely interested in being your friend to actually try. In some cases, you may find that people would not be as cruel as you suspect if you actually tried being around them more. If people do stay away from you, it may not be because they think you're gross or weird, but because they're afraid of accidentally saying something that will hurt your feelings.

. . . AND SIGNS YOU AREN'T:

You know you're not imagining things because you've heard or experienced the nasty things your classmates have said or done, both to your face and behind your back.

WHAT YOUR PARENTS SAY TO TRY TO HELP:

"If you want to win your battle against a tough illness, you have to be tough yourself," or "If you'd just be more positive about your illness, you'd have more positive results," or "If kids are teasing you, it's because they don't understand your illness, so just explain it to them and I'm sure you'll be fast friends."

. . . AND WHY IT ISN'T HELPFUL AT ALL:

Despite what everyone says, most illnesses aren't battles, they're ambushes. While it's important to be tough in order to manage your illness, being tough won't make your illness disappear. So implying that toughness and positivity will make your condition go away will only set you up to blame yourself for not accomplishing the impossible.

WHAT YOU THINK YOU NEED TO FIGURE OUT IN ORDER TO FIX IT:

If there's no way to make your symptoms better, you wish there were some way to just be more confident and less bothered by and envious of the healthy people around you. If you could just convince yourself to be cool about your situation and friendly to everyone, you could convince classmates that you're normal and the kind of person they'd want to be friends with.

WHY THOSE FIXES WILL FAIL:

Trying to change your feelings hasn't made a difference because it hasn't made them go away. All it's done is make you obsess even more about your illness and find more ways to blame yourself for things that aren't your fault at all, such as having severe allergies and how self-conscious and unhappy they make you feel. The harder you try to be a "real person," the more fake you feel, which means you aren't buying it and neither is anyone else. And pretending to be normal isn't just difficult, it's dangerous, because you're increasing your risk of doing something that will make your condition worse.

WHAT YOU CAN ACTUALLY DO ABOUT IT:

First, learn everything there is to know about your illness, like its risks and effects and how to plan for emergencies. Try to find people with the same condition who can act as a support group, either through your doctor or parents or possibly on message boards online. Yes, it's scary to investigate, but use your fear to ask questions and seek answers, not just about how to manage your illness but how to live well in spite of it. Once you know you're doing your best to manage your situation, you'll be ready to protect yourself from the fears and criticism of others. And you may find friends who appreciate your strength.

RED FLAGS TO LOOK FOR IN THE FUTURE:

If you find yourself thinking of nothing but your symptoms and how to stop them, ignoring the really important stuff you want to do with your life, or seeking relief by doing whatever makes you feel good regardless of how dangerous it is, then you are in trouble.

THE UN-SUGARCOATED SUCKINESS YOU CAN EXPECT:

Your illness may be a lifelong condition, even if it lies low for long periods. So even though it's the one causing the trouble, it's connected to you, so you're responsible for taking care of yourself and suffering the consequences if you don't.

THE UNTRUE SUCKINESS YOU MUST REJECT:

Even if your best efforts at managing symptoms fail, that doesn't mean that you've failed. Symptoms that are getting worse are never signs of failure. If your disorder leaves you stuck with pain, embarrassment, and problems getting work done, you should always judge yourself by what you do despite these factors and not by what the symptoms do to you or how effective you are at stopping them. If you can focus on and pursue the things in life that truly matter to you and that you actually have some control over—like being a good friend, an honest person, or the best dog trainer possible (why not?), as opposed to being happy, attractive, and pain-free—then no symptoms will ever be able to control or define you.

WHEN YOUR LOOKS MAKE YOU SICK: A GUIDE TO APPEARANCE- AND BODY-RELATED DISORDERS

In this chapter, we often try to warn you that becoming obsessed with your appearance can lead you to make dangerous compromises when it comes to your health. We also frequently mention how the best way to protect yourself in risky situations is through doing your research, so you can know where the true risks lie and make smarter decisions. So, with both of those ideas in mind, and with some actual medical knowledge (since one of the authors is an MD), we thought we'd do some of the research for you and go into more detail about the very real dangers of becoming too fixated on or negative about your looks.

For some people, such fixations are more annoying than risky. For too many others, however, the drive to be thin or beautiful can literally make them crazy. At that point, they're not just obsessed, they're sick with an eating disorder that has a mind of its own and can be very hard to recover from. And because such illnesses are also stigmatized, not only is it hard for people to learn the truth about them, it is also difficult for people suffering from them to seek help.

Of course, just knowing about the dangers of certain activities isn't guaranteed to save you from engaging in them, especially if you have a family history of addiction or compulsive behavior. But knowledge is always power, not only when it comes to learning the facts about eating disorders, but about the truth beyond the stigma. Just because you have a few powerful unwanted thoughts doesn't mean you're crazy or broken. Nobody's totally in control of how they think, but we can all refuse to buy into the stigma of mental illness.

Here are the hard facts about some of the specific risks from becoming overly obsessed with your looks. Hopefully, knowing these risks can make it easier to get help or, even better, to avoid falling prey to these obsessions entirely.

DISORDER: BODY DYSMORPHIA

What it means in basic terms: Your brain gives you a warped, negative, unrealistic perception of what you look like. So no matter how good you really look, you can only see a hideous monster.

Symptoms: Inability to feel good about how you

look, despite all your friends, family, available medical professionals, and friends and followers on social media trying to tell you otherwise.

Risks to your health: Aside from the drag of always feeling bad about yourself, body dysmorphia is a big part of all the other disorders listed here.

Treatment/General effectiveness: You can't stop the wild ideas your brain sends you about food and your body. But you can learn to control your actions and get support for keeping the overwhelming thoughts from taking over. Dialectical Behavior Therapy (DBT), which can be taught by therapists, counselors, or through workbooks you can use on your own, can help you manage the negative and harmful feelings. It's also useful for managing self-destructive eating disorder behaviors overall.

DISORDER: ANOREXIA

What it means in basic terms: You can't see past the body dysmorphia previously described, and you become convinced that you're disgustingly fat. You can't stop starving yourself and finding other ways to lose weight.

Symptoms: An obsession with thinness, a fear of food, and a feeling of self-disgust when you eat. No matter how little you eat and how (frighteningly) thin you get, you're never happy with how you look or convinced that eating will do anything but make you feel awful.

Risks to your health: While the initial risks include anemia, passing out, losing bone density, and messing up the rhythm of your heart, the biggest risk is, terrifyingly, death.

Treatment/General effectiveness: After a little self-education, you and your parents will know how to find treatment and how to tell when the danger of death is so great that you need to be in a hospital. Treatment in a hospital may not improve your attitude toward your appearance or food. However, it can keep you safe by controlling your behavior and it can offer you tools for doing better when you get out. Your goal isn't to fix the way you see yourself and eating, but to be strong enough to stay out of danger and go on with your life.

DISORDER: BULIMIA

What it means in basic terms: Like anorexia, except instead of starving yourself, you eat normally, or overeat, and then, overwhelmed with fear and self-disgust, force yourself to throw up.

Symptoms: Your weight will probably be normal (and certainly never on the dangerously thin side). But it becomes harder to avoid overeating once you've gotten into the habit of bingeing, which means it also becomes hard to stop throwing up afterward.

Risks to your health: Because bulimia doesn't cause sufferers to look as sick and gaunt as anorexics do, many people don't think bulimia's that dangerous. However, depriving your body of necessary nutrients, no matter how you do it, may do serious damage. On top of that, vomiting repeatedly erodes your teeth (and ruins your breath) with stomach acid. More dangerously, it can also cause dangerous heart rhythms by changing the chemical balance of your blood.

Treatment/General effectiveness: As with anorexia, educate yourself so that you and your parents can find treatment and recognize when you're in enough danger that you need to check into the hospital. Outpatient treatments are the same as they are for anorexia, as is the fact that people with bulimia can lead healthy lives, once they get over the shame of having a disorder.

DISORDER: ORTHOREXIA

What it means in basic terms: An intense obsession with diet and exercise, like a food-based OCD. It's often part of anorexia, but it can also stand on its own.

Symptoms: Many strict, sometimes arbitrary rules about what you can and cannot eat, how much you have to exercise, and an irrational feeling that, if you do not stick to these rules, something truly terrible and scary will happen.

Risks to your health: Aside from excessive weight loss and all the damage that comes with that (as previously described), there's the overall damage to your well-being that OCD and anxiety disorders can cause.

Treatment/General effectiveness: If you can gain the perspective to see that your obsessions are ruining your life, you can look for a therapist and/or a group that will strengthen that perspective and help you limit the time and energy taken up by obsessional exercise and dieting.

DISORDER: SELF-HARM

What it means in basic terms: Hurting yourself by doing anything from starving to cutting yourself to overdosing, in order to "relieve" depression or anxiety.

Symptoms: Visible external signs of damage, from being too thin to having cuts and burn scars on your forearms, thighs, or elsewhere.

Risks to your health: Damaging your skin is rarely fatal, but the scars can, of course, be permanent. An overdose, however, can undermine your goals and relationships and possibly kill you.

Treatment/General effectiveness: No treatment is guaranteed to stop self-harm or change an impulsive temperament, but DBT (as previously described) is an effective management tool.

SECTION 2

BODIES SUCK...
When You're the Wrong Size

SINCE IT'S ONE OF THE most obvious physical traits, size is often the first measurement we use to define "normal" weight. And being a non-average size (compared to the prevailing standard) can make us feel uneasy about ourselves and others. We can't help having those feelings any more than we can change our size overnight. But we can learn how to prevent negative feelings and insecurity about our size from controlling the way we value ourselves and choose our friends. And as for those who are uncomfortable with our size—which, frankly, is most of us—we can learn how to work around the haters until they either grow up or we move on to better things.

HERE'S AN EXAMPLE:

I shouldn't feel different because I'm fat, because my whole family is overweight and my parents have never given me a hard time about it. They've always encouraged me to love the way I look. The problem is that I can't just stay at home. And I can't avoid gym class, or feeling like crap when nothing fits me at the stores. I'm funny—certainly when it comes to making fun of myself—and bend over backward to be nice. So I manage not to get picked on as much as I used to be. It still hurts, though, because most people only think of me as a funny fat kid, not as a real person. So aside from my two very close best friends, nobody ever invites me to hang out or go to their parties. I hate the feeling of being different and wish that there were something I could do about it, or that at least I could figure out how to get over the way I look and what people think about it.

SIGNS YOU MAY BE MISINTERPRETING THINGS:

Your self-consciousness could be making you a little

paranoid. Others may not be able to ignore your physical differences, but that doesn't mean they're as fixated on them as you are. Or you could be taking your own bad feelings about how you look and unfairly projecting them onto others. In other words, other people probably notice that you're bigger than they are, but it's possible they are way more comfortable with your differences than you are.

. . . AND SIGNS YOU AREN'T:

You would absolutely be comfortable with those differences if people around you weren't making an obvious effort to constantly remind you that you look different and should feel bad about it. You've overheard and seen their nasty comments. And your friends have heard and seen it all, too.

WHAT YOUR PARENTS SAY TO TRY TO HELP:

"Projecting confidence is the ultimate beauty secret," or "The key to looking good is feeling good—love your looks and everyone else will fall in line!" or "It's inner beauty that really counts; if these kids got to know you, they'd know you're great."

. . . AND WHY IT ISN'T HELPFUL AT ALL:

Most times, if you put yourself out there, the jerks are

the first people to notice and sometimes pounce with nasty comments. So, while you think it's true that you look better when you feel better about yourself, nice smiles often attract meanness from not-nice people more than they attract friendship from nice ones. As for your inner beauty, it varies according to your mood and the crap you have to deal with, neither of which you control. And unfortunately, you've never been impressed with humankind's ability to choose inner beauty over the outward kind.

WHAT YOU THINK YOU NEED TO FIGURE OUT IN ORDER TO FIX IT:

You'd like to find a magical solution that would make you look like everyone else. You search for talents or activities that will get people to overlook your appearance and notice your personality. In place of that, you'd take a transfer to another school, state, or planet where people are less judgmental or where fixing your physical issues will somehow be easier. If nothing else, you'd take anything that would get you to like yourself more or just obsess less over your looks and the impression they leave on others.

WHY THOSE FIXES WILL FAIL:

You've said and done everything possible to get kids to laugh with you, not at you, and you just can't do it better. And the more you watch TV and movies or just exist in the world, the more you notice that people's reactions to bodies that are big, short, curvy, and anything else other than thin remain unfair. You've tried changing something, but you can't change the thing about how you look that makes you feel not-normal. And that just usually draws more unwanted attention from jerks who are all too happy to remind you that the one thing they love to torment you about hasn't gone anywhere. In fact, doing anything just to get approval from other people, especially your tormentors, only gives their negativity more power over you. It makes no sense to care the most about pleasing and impressing the people who care about you the least.

WHAT YOU CAN ACTUALLY DO ABOUT IT:

If something about your appearance is too unusual to go unnoticed, it may be almost impossible to easily find general acceptance. In time, however, finding a more accepting group is both possible and worthwhile, as long as you don't let loneliness and the desire to belong to the "normal" group encourage you to reject yourself. Once you've found an accepting group, or a close friend or two, that is authentic and has your back, it makes it easier to dismiss the opinions of the ignorant jerks who don't. And whenever you hear criticism, either from jerks or from the meanest recesses of your own head, remind yourself that you're doing nothing wrong and everything right while making the best of a tough situation. Ultimately, it's knowing that you're doing your best, not whether you're looking or feeling your best, that can give you the confidence to respond to would-be hurtful comments. By being forced to stand up for who you really are, apart from your looks, you're developing strength that will help you find real friends and survive not just school but life in general.

RED FLAGS TO LOOK FOR IN THE FUTURE:

Putting too much value on looks may distract you from more important, less superficial things. It may also drive you to hate yourself to the point where love and friendship can't make you feel better. If you become convinced that your apperance makes you worthless, then you're really in trouble, because you won't value yourself enough to care about doing the right thing or even keeping yourself safe. Most importantly, be careful not to become so fixated on what other people say about your looks that you develop obsessive, unhealthy habits, like starving or even cutting yourself, which are dangerous and extremely destructive.

THE UN-SUGARCOATED SUCKINESS YOU CAN EXPECT:

You may sometimes be unable to avoid twinges of envy and self-criticism when comparing yourself to people who you think are more attractive, happier, and well liked. (That's just human nature.) And you may feel that those people are distancing themselves from you because they are more attractive, happier, and well liked. That's bound to make you feel hurt, rejected, and lonely. There is pain when people respond more strongly to your appearance than to your character and personality, or when you, yourself, can't stop having such thoughts. Sucky as it may be, you can never expect yourself to completely control that pain or those thoughts and make them disappear.

THE UNTRUE SUCKINESS YOU MUST REJECT:

Don't let your feelings of pain, difference, or inferiority make you believe that you're a failure or cause you to make dangerous compromises in order to feel better.

Your job is not to make yourself happy. Your job is to do your best to make friends, keep learning, and be a decent person, despite the self-doubt, self-hate, and rejection, and take pride in that accomplishment. You may not ever be able to feel totally good or comfortable about your appearance—lots of people don't—but if you can push beyond that doubt and keep doing what's positive, your appearance will become less and less important as you get stronger in the ways that count.

We Attempt to Explain . . .
That "Fat" Is Not an Insult

It's natural to assume that being fat, or just being called fat, is a bad thing. After all, being thin and muscular has become the acceptable and ideal body type, especially for women. More than two in three American adults are considered to be overweight or obese, but judging from the people you see on TV, in movies, and in advertising, you'd think that your average American is tall, skinny, and in shape, and anyone who looks different is a freak.

Those who believe that thinness

is superior often insist that it doesn't just look better, but it's always better for you. After all, there are some very real health risks that go along with being overweight, like diabetes and heart disease. And since, as the common wisdom goes, anyone can lose weight through diet and exercise, fat people deserve to be mocked for their poor decisions and laziness.

Until the last century, an average person's food supply wasn't as consistent, convenient, or abundant as it is now, so people who stored weight easily were the ones who survived and passed their genes on. Since food is now everywhere, often in cheap, fast, and fatty or sweet forms, our food-storing cells are now less of a gift and more of a burden (since they leave us with more of a gut). So the genes that once saved our ancestors by helping them store fat now may make us miserable.

Accepting the truth about fatness isn't easy, especially—and ironically—if you're overweight yourself. And as any overweight person knows, being told that you're not fat when you are is actually hurtful, because you're being told that the thing you are—that who you are—is so wrong that it must be denied at all costs.

Even if it's hard to accept how you look, it's necessary to accept that weight has no real connection to intelligence, willpower, or character. And the more scientists learn about DNA, the clearer it becomes that much about our appearance is determined by our genes, not by our consumption of salad. Furthermore, while obesity can be bad for your well-being, not every overweight person is sick or at risk of diabetes, just as not every thin person has a perfect bill of health. There's nothing wrong with trying to be healthy and fit into skinny jeans, but unless you've got actual skinny genes, pushing yourself to become and stay very thin can often be anything but.

Ultimately, the healthiest thing you can do is to stop seeing fatness as a sin and being called fat as a slur even if people mean it that way. Our culture may tell us that it's better to be thin, or even that it's wrong to be fat. But we need to start telling ourselves the truth—that weight is a fairly neutral characteristic, like the color of your eyes or the hand you write with. In other words, no matter what the media or the mean kids tell you, being fat isn't any worse than being green-eyed or right-handed. It just is, and while knowing that won't stop you from feeling hurt when teased, it can help you fight the self-hate and shame that teasing brings. As such, the best way to outwardly react to anyone who wants to make you feel ashamed of your size shouldn't be with hurt or anger, just indifference. Since there's nothing wrong with being big, someone who calls you fat isn't so much teasing you as demonstrating that he's not blind or that he's just fond of stating the obvious.

You don't have to love the way you look—most people don't love their own looks—but you don't have to be ashamed of your body, either. There's no reason to be—and those who can't stop dumping on uncontrollable natural differences deserve your pity, not scorn, because you'd rather be fat than an idiot.

BODIES SUCK . . .

When You Look "Wrong"

SO MUCH ABOUT HOW WE look is out of our control. However, if the issue with your appearance is something that happened to you, rather than something you were born with, the way people react can be extra weird. They often assume that you can and should do something to fix it, if only because they're afraid it could happen to them just like it randomly happened to you. But it's not your job to change the way you look or to protect other people from their fears. It's your job to stay true to your own values and beliefs, to live with the undeserved pain that life can sometimes dump on you for no reason at all, and to protect yourself from the ugliness of superficial people.

HERE'S AN EXAMPLE:

I never used to notice my looks or my friends' looks. But now I have psoriasis (a red, disgusting skin rash that I obviously hate), so things are different. At first, everyone started to joke about how it was contagious. But it wasn't funny, and some of my friends stopped hanging out with me. Since then, I've gotten quiet and just avoid people. I don't see the point in caring about my body now that my face is so gross that nobody would ever want to be with me, anyway. Right now I feel like I'm always going to be a lonely, unhappy person who avoids other people. All I want is to find a way back to the way I was.

SIGNS YOU MAY BE MISINTERPRETING THINGS:

It's possible that you're projecting your own self-consciousness about your looks onto others. Or you might be depressed about this issue, and that depression about your appearance, not your appearance itself, is what's driving people away.

. . . AND SIGNS YOU AREN'T:

The friends who have your back confirm that you aren't just being sensitive. And the ones who used to are clearly acting different now and have backed away, despite your efforts to be friendly and act like nothing's wrong. You know you haven't imagined the way people stay away from you at lunch or talk to one another about parties that you're never invited to.

WHAT YOUR PARENTS SAY TO TRY TO HELP:

"If these kids aren't smart enough not to judge a book by its cover, then they're not worth having as friends," or "If the way you look is getting this kind of attention, then don't draw attention to it," or "If you're being true to yourself, then who cares what anyone else says?"

. . . AND WHY IT ISN'T HELPFUL AT ALL:

People can't stop themselves from judging a book by its cover, and you can't stop yourself from missing friends who were once close to you or from liking them and from wanting to be friends again in spite of their superficial, cover-deep stupidity. So if you get rejected because your appearance is too "different," you can't hold yourself responsible for people's bad judgment or for the pain of rejection or losing friends you were once close to. You've probably done everything you can to improve how you look, and changing it further is impossible. And if you've made changes to your looks on purpose but hate the way they bring you unwanted attention, then changing would require you to compromise and reject who you really are.

WHAT YOU THINK YOU NEED TO FIGURE OUT IN ORDER TO FIX IT:

You wish for that secret combination of confidence and cool that will allow you to love yourself enough to ignore others, but still get them to see and recognize the real you.

WHY THOSE FIXES WILL FAIL:

You haven't found any quick fixes for your confidence, especially since it's constantly taking hits whenever kids show you no respect or no interest in getting to know you. You don't see how you could be more immune to negativity since ignoring bullies only seems to make them more determined.

WHAT YOU CAN ACTUALLY DO ABOUT IT:

Once you're sure that you've done everything you can to reach out, forgive your old friends' fears and prejudices, and try to restore your old relationships, your job is to accept loss and rejection as an unavoidable part of life's eternal suckiness that may not go away soon. You can also acknowledge that their inability to like or just relate to you isn't personal—their bias comes from a mix of ignorance and an incapability for kindness. Moments of feeling humiliated or disrespected may be inevitable, but they're worth enduring in order to get as much from school and life as you can. Even if you can't stop feeling hurt or having bad thoughts, you can, with a therapist's help, learn to challenge those thoughts to lessen their impact. It may help to keep a mental list of brief responses to worst-case insults (particularly the ones you tell yourself) that flatly, clearly, and emotionlessly establish your lack of interest. There's nothing wrong with hanging out with your family if you enjoy it, so make maximum use of them for friendship and support.

RED FLAGS TO LOOK FOR IN THE FUTURE:

Watch out if you find yourself obsessing about your appearance, especially if that obsession cuts into time better spent doing productive things you actually like and trying to be a good person. While it's not dangerous to feel angry, self-critical, hurt, or lonely, it is unhealthy to let those feelings keep you focused on the people who put down your looks and made you feel that way. They may demand some of your attention, but you have to be careful not to give them more than the bare minimum in order to limit their power to torment you, define you, and push you to become bitter. It's also dangerous to believe that you'll never be happy or do worthwhile things simply because you're hurting now and can't stop it. Life may be painful and unfair sometimes, but it's what you do at those times that makes it worth living, not what it does to you.

THE UN-SUGARCOATED SUCKINESS YOU CAN EXPECT:

Given the mean attacks on your appearance, you may have to constantly fight the feeling that life in general is a lonely, unfair toilet. And the toilety feeling can be worse if you once thought you were great at managing your life before bad luck changed everything. There's no real way to make other people shut up and leave you alone, so you'll have to expect more nasty comments, or at least the possibility of them, and a harder road ahead than others have overall.

THE UNTRUE SUCKINESS YOU MUST REJECT:

Don't accept the blame for being unable to look more "normal" or to get others to be more accepting and less cruel. And don't expect to be able to solve your appearance issues when you can't. You may be forced to deal with jerks on a regular basis and with lonely thoughts when you're left out of social events, but jerks and loneliness can't totally stop you from living your life on your terms. They don't have the power to prevent you from finding things you want to do and people you want to do them with. Looking different automatically enrolls you in an unofficial survival course in how to live with unfair treatment. And if you stay focused on emerging from this period with your hope, faith in real friendship, and determination to do good things intact, you'll pass this course with flying colors.

BODIES SUCK: THE POINT

People have strong and often negative reactions to bodies that differ from society's arbitrary norms. And there's not much you can do to stop anyone, be it other people or your own mind, from openly expressing those reactions, no matter how unkind, unreasonable, and generally un-okay they may sometimes be. But you can learn to tell the difference between intense negative feelings that seem like valid criticisms but aren't, and legitimate judgments that come from your own experience and values. Then there'll be nothing to stop you from pursuing your goals and living up to your values regardless of the criticism or rejection of others or bad feelings inside yourself. Remember to value the things that are more important but don't necessarily make you feel good, like how hard you work and how decently you treat people. If you can tolerate falling short of the physical standard and still pursue your own way forward, not only are you likely to find good friends in the future, but also be the kind of person who can help other people, and the world, be better.

CHAPTER FIVE

HOMES SUCK

PROBLEMS INVOLVING YOUR FAMILY CAN extend far beyond the walls of your house. Not only do they get all the way into your head, but they can also go further to create difficulties at school, with friends, and in every corner of your world.

The issues created by an unstable or unconventional home are as varied as they are personal. And it's because they're so personal that their negative effects can spread so far. That's why when we talk about "problems at home" we're actually talking about "problems with the universe" and the kinds of personal issues that no house could ever contain.

What makes home-related conflicts so difficult to resolve is how nearly impossible they are for anyone to control. And conflict is almost impossible to stop once it starts. A lot of the time, conflict within one's home is especially irresolvable because the parties involved are married or otherwise related, and are determined to stay together and make things work. And they will fight to do this, even if they still fight each other.

Sometimes the conflict isn't within the home but outside it, such as a family having to deal with not being accepted by the community they happen to live in. The issues they're coping with are just as unsolvable and feel just as personal and overwhelming.

Of course, uncontrollable problems do have an upside. It's painful and infuriating to have to deal with a problem that nobody can fix. But that almost always means that there's nobody to blame and no reason to feel responsible for making things better. Accepting this fact is difficult, but once you do, life will become a whole lot easier.

It's hard to come to terms with the inability to fix family problems. We often falsely believe that we should be able to make these things better and are a failure if we can't. And when our family is the source of pain, it makes us, as a member of that family, feel like there's also a problem with who *we* are and where we come from.

Despite the assumption that everyone needs a happy home life in order to grow up into a strong, normal, and happy adult, many people who grow up in unhappy homes do just fine. That's because learning how to live with pain and unhappiness teaches us a huge deal about life. It also helps build character as much as a supportive home would. And, on the other side of the happiness tracks, happy childhood homes can often create dangers later on, such as super-high expectations for happiness and a feeling of failure if, despite all their reasons to be happy, people's bad luck makes happiness impossible.

Living in a broken or unhappy home, or just coming from a family that breaks the mold, may make you feel a special type of terrible. And it's hard to accept that the broken parts of your family can't be fixed. But once you accept that you shouldn't take responsibility for fixing it, you can focus on the goals that are actually within your power and find a way forward. You're not giving up on your family, just on making your family functional, accepted, or whole. Most importantly, you're not giving up on yourself and the kind of person you want to become, regardless of the home you started in.

HOW TO FIGURE OUT FOR YOURSELF WHAT MAKES A HOME SUCK

The adjectives most frequently used to describe the quality of one's home life are *happy* and *unhappy*. So you'd think that the best way to judge what your home is like is by how it makes you feel. But some people are content with their families, even though they're going through tough problems. Other people are stressed and miserable at home even though their families are functioning fairly well. If you can figure out your own objective standards for how serious your home problems are, and not overreact to whether they make you feel tuned out or overwhelmed, you will become more effective at figuring out what you can and can't do to make things better and dealing with family problems while keeping an eye on your own priorities. Here's a quiz to help you be more objective about where your family is on the happy–unhappy scale.

1 Your father has just returned home after a long, hard, particularly terrible day at his job (which he hates). You expect his next course of action will be to:

A) Immediately start yelling at the first person unlucky enough to cross his path, followed by some door-slamming and more yelling.

B) Talk it out a bit with your other parent or disappear into his room/office/bathroom for a while to unwind. Then sit down to dinner and start acting like his normal self or at least a quieter version.

C) Act normally, which means cheerful and chatty because adult problems are too much for you and your siblings to handle.

2 **Every so often, your father has one of what he calls his "low times." You see these times as:**

A) Sad for him but pretty awesome for you as you can pretty much do whatever you want when your mom's at work.

B) Really tough, because you, your mom, and your siblings aren't always great at dealing with chores around the house and it's hard to see your dad so unhappy. In other words, it's not impossible to deal with, but it's not easy, either.

C) Not fair, because dads aren't supposed to take a day off and kids aren't supposed to do dads' jobs.

3 **Your parents have been fighting every night after dinner for the past two weeks. You don't really know what the fights are about because they're quiet at first, but by the time they start yelling, it's clear that they can't stand each other. Your take on this is:**

A) That it's only worth paying attention to if they start breaking things, so you might as well listen to music on your headphones for now. If it really starts to get distracting then that's the perfect excuse to ignore your homework and go visit a friend.

B) To get yourself and your siblings to the quietest part of the house, play some music to cover your parents' yelling, and try to ignore it. If the fights keep happening, however, you'll find a time to talk to one of your parents to let them know how it's affecting the family and ask what, if anything, you can do to help.

C) This would never happen, because all it would take is ten minutes of raised voices before you would lose your mind and call 911.

4 Your sister has been making your life a living hell for the past month. She's been taking your stuff without asking, punching you, and trashing your schoolwork. And neither of your parents is taking it seriously or doing anything about it. To you, this situation is:

A) Fine, because your parents are busy people, life is hard, and you'll get her to cut it out yourself someday, when you're older, taller, and it's payback time!

B) Not okay because of how much it messes with your ability to get work done, relax, and generally live your life. So if you can't have a serious talk with your parents and let them know you need their help, you're going to have to find a way to not be at home so much.

C) So unbearable and severe that you're willing to contact the FBI or hire a hit man in order to make it stop.

ANSWER KEY

IF YOUR ANSWERS WERE MAINLY As:

You expect too little structure and safety from home. You're so used to turmoil at home that you're fine just lying low, looking out for yourself, and putting distance between yourself and your family whenever things get rough. But having to take care of yourself may mean that you ignore your education and avoid making plans because you don't want to make waves. Not expecting much may seem to make life easier, but disconnecting from your family and just getting through life means you're losing focus on being the kind of person you want to be.

IF YOUR ANSWERS WERE MAINLY Bs:

You expect just enough from home. When it comes to the turmoil at home, you're neither too accepting nor too easily rattled. You are able to keep track of your own goals while staying engaged with your family and ready to find ways to help everyone work together. You stay focused on your own plans for moving ahead in life, despite whatever's going on with your life at home.

IF YOUR ANSWERS WERE MAINLY Cs:

You expect too much structure and safety at home. You feel sensitive to family conflict and hate the way your family doesn't come up with solutions. Difficult situations fill you with feelings of helplessness and anger, and you have a need to set things right, no matter what it takes. If you can't fix things, you sometimes panic, even though the fix is often not your responsibility or within your control. And the panic only makes the problem worse. It's hard to think of realistic solutions when you constantly feel like your world is out of control.

SECTION 1

HOMES SUCK . . .
When Everybody's Always Fighting

WHEN PEOPLE IN YOUR HOUSE are fighting, it can feel less like a home and more like a battlefield. Anyone who enters should have their guard up and seek cover. But these aren't fights you can win, even with big guns and a battle plan. So your goal isn't to become mean enough to survive or even clever enough to make the fighting stop. Your goal is to focus on your own priorities and keep the war in your house from getting into your head.

HERE'S AN EXAMPLE:

There are classmates at school I really like. But I can't ever get that close to anyone because I don't want anyone to ask or know about what it's like at home. It feels like my parents don't love, or even really like, each other anymore. They fight a lot, which makes my mom cry. And since I'm the oldest, I end up being the one trying to keep the peace (or at least trying to keep my younger siblings from getting into the line of fire). So I'm just not comfortable with making friends since I'm usually stressed, exhausted, and wanting to keep quiet. And I'm not close enough to anyone to talk about what I'm going through, so I have to keep it all to myself. I don't see a way out of this situation at home, but I wish there were still some way for me to make real friends and be happy.

SIGNS YOU MAY BE MISINTERPRETING THINGS:

It's always possible that you're oversensitive to the raised voices and conflict that may come with an emotionally intense family. You may also be anxious or worried about rejection, which can put a dark filter over your ability to perceive and judge how kids at school would react if they knew what it was like for you at home.

. . . AND SIGNS YOU AREN'T:

You aren't normally bothered by loud-talkers as long as they're not yelling at you. You trust your ability to know when people are angry, whether they're mad at you or anyone else. So you trust your reading of the stormy weather report over your house.

WHAT YOUR PARENTS SAY TO TRY TO HELP:

"I know we're having a tough time, but that's why you need to be as good as gold right now, okay?" or "Stop making this about you—you're just making things worse!" or "If you'd stop trying to help, everything would be fine!"

. . . AND WHY IT ISN'T HELPFUL AT ALL:

When there's tension at home, most children know not to rock the boat. But sometimes they can't help it. So unless you've got the sweetest, calmest temperament in the world, you can't help but speak up about how much you hate the situation and want it to stop. And it's worse when you're ignored, criticized, or treated unfairly when you raise the topic of what's going on at home. So being asked to be extra good just adds to your stress. It also adds to your stress because you feel partly to blame for causing your parents to fight more if you do misbehave.

WHAT YOU THINK YOU NEED TO FIGURE OUT IN ORDER TO FIX IT:

You've been told that you need to stay out of it and be

a nicer person, but you struggle to find ways to make that happen. You may also want to limit the conflict by figuring out a way to just get along and do whatever it takes, from forcing them into therapy to finding a magic spell, to keep the peace and make things fair.

WHY THOSE FIXES WILL FAIL:

No matter how often adults tell you that you have choices about how you behave, everyone's self-control has its limits. And when you've tried as hard as you can to be a nice, agreeable person without success, you risk becoming angry, disagreeable, and guilt-ridden. And the same goes for trying to change other people or fix the situation. Because if you thought controlling your own feelings and behavior was hard, you'll soon realize that trying to control or change the way others feel and behave is downright impossible.

WHAT YOU CAN ACTUALLY DO ABOUT IT:

When you're living in a war zone, it's nearly impossible to live a normal life. While classmates are thinking about seeing friends and having fun, you're just thinking about surviving dinner and having a second to yourself to relax. That's why your main focus shouldn't be about being happy, but on being a good person despite the bad things going on under your roof. And as much as it hurts to know you can't fix things or make yourself feel better, it's also a relief because that means you're not to blame or a failure because your family life is hell. Your job is to take good care of yourself while helping your family if you can. And that might mean anything from cooking and cleaning, to caring for your siblings, to getting a part-time job. But in the meantime, remember your own needs. Find time for the important stuff, like extracurriculars, homework, and your hobbies. Trying to be helpful, to not overreact to everyone else's unhappiness, and to keep your own life on track may never feel very good. But every day that you avoid getting discouraged by what's going on at home brings you closer to your own goals.

RED FLAGS TO LOOK FOR IN THE FUTURE:

It may be almost impossible not to feel stressed and angry. But you have to be careful not to let that anger push you to vent your frustration and find a way to "get even." While it's also hard not to constantly focus on your family, don't let that make you forget about your own goals and how to reach them. You should also avoid the temptation to escape the situation with behavior that will get you into trouble.

THE UN-SUGARCOATED SUCKINESS YOU CAN EXPECT:

There may be no way you can stop the fighting, protect your siblings, or generally make your home, family, and life as peaceful and sane as you wish they could be. You may find yourself constantly frightened or angry, instead of worried about normal stuff. And it may be hard to fight off feelings of resentment, exhaustion, and defeat.

THE UNTRUE SUCKINESS YOU MUST REJECT:

Your family may be a hot mess, your house may be off-limits to friends, and your bedroom may be the only place in the world you can get a second of peace. But that doesn't mean you're a loser, a freak, or anything but a regular person with the bad luck of being in a bad situation at the moment. Remember, you have no control over the stability or happiness of your family or even of your own feelings. But when you're able to be a good person, help out when possible, and stay focused on your own work, despite living in chaos, you're accomplishing something incredible.

DO MY FRIENDS/COUNSELORS HAVE A POINT?

WHEN YOUR FRIENDS/COUNSELORS SAY . . .

"Are you sure you're not making too big of a deal over what might just be normal family fighting, discipline, or conflict?"

IT SOUNDS DUMB BECAUSE . . .

You've already asked yourself this question hundreds of times. Eventually, after admitting to yourself that there's no room for misinterpretation, you came to trust your perception of things and you wish they'd see it your way.

BUT IT'S NOT DUMB TO THEM BECAUSE . . .

It's likely that they do trust you, but, like you, they don't want to believe this is happening or has happened. Not only don't they want to accept that something like this could happen to you, they also know that intervening in a family conflict is a big deal.

SO BE SMART AND . . .

Don't let the feeling of being misunderstood or having your concerns disregarded make you think that people don't care about you or are unwilling to believe what you have to say.

THEN RESPOND BY . . .

Agreeing that it's important not to overreact. Which is why you've already given the whole thing so much thought. Then spell out the facts as you know them as plainly and unemotionally as possible. That way, they'll be able to see not just where you're coming from, but how strong, brave, and justified you are in saying what needs to be said.

We Attempt to Explain . . .
"The Nuclear Option"

If you're in a situation at home or at school that's putting you in danger, or if you know someone in a situation like that, it's common to feel scared, lost, and, worst of all, trapped. Going to the authorities for help—also known as "the nuclear option"—usually seems way too intimidating or risky to even try. In fact, people use this term not because no one should choose this option, but because of how intense and intimidating taking this step can be.

But if your situation is putting you in danger and you haven't been able to find a way to fix it, it's important to know that the nuclear option is available to you and what pursuing it actually means. That way, you won't spook yourself out of taking it if necessary, nor will you be caught off guard by what happens next.

Generally speaking, taking the nuclear option in cases

of abuse at home or at school means going to "mandated reporters," such as teachers, counselors, or doctors, or reporting directly to law enforcement. They will alert the proper authorities so they can do an investigation and make sure everyone is safe.

And yes, the results are sometimes nuclear in terms of having people you know and love explode with anger, frustration, and blame. But an investigation is often the only way to save young people from horrible situations and, frequently, save parents from themselves.

Even if reporting an abusive situation has results you didn't want or expect, hurts people you love, or makes your life more difficult in other ways, *you should never blame yourself*. You were forced to choose the nuclear option because of an awful situation you did not (and do not) choose to be in and can't be held responsible for. So refuse to allow anyone to make you feel like what's happening to you is your fault.

Don't ever hesitate to tell trusted adults about potential abuse and don't let yourself feel responsible if people you love are upset by what happens next. Be proud of whatever you do to restore safety. You're not responsible for the explosion if there is one, and you should be proud of doing what's necessary to protect yourself and others from the original danger.

HOMES SUCK . . .
When Your Home Is Scary

WHEN YOUR HOME ISN'T JUST turbulent but terrifying, your whole world is thrown into chaos. Focusing on anything but survival can feel impossible. You may feel desperate, helpless, and paralyzed, but those feelings are almost always misguided. Just because you feel afraid and anxious doesn't mean that you are actually paralyzed or unable to make things better. There are almost always opportunities to make your life better and yourself stronger.

HERE'S AN EXAMPLE:

I always thought we had a happy family until my father came home one night and said that his business was going under and we were going to lose everything. Suddenly, we had to sell our house and a bunch of our stuff and move to a tiny apartment where my sister and I have to share a room. Now my parents are always arguing about everything, especially money, but they also take out a lot of their frustration on my sister and me, like this is our fault somehow. Sure, we need stuff for school—and life in general—but that's not exactly our choice. Plus I don't really have anyone to talk to about what's going on since my friends all disappeared. I think they're all freaked out by what happened and just don't know what to say. In the meantime, I don't know how much longer I can deal with this and I really don't know how to make it better.

SIGNS YOU MAY BE MISINTERPRETING THINGS:

As discussed before, you might be an especially anxious, oversensitive person. But when you're dealing with really scary situations like these, they're hard for anyone to misjudge.

. . . AND SIGNS YOU AREN'T:

You know what it feels like to be terrified and screamed at.

WHAT YOUR PARENTS SAY TO TRY TO HELP:

"I wouldn't act this way if you weren't always messing up and trying to make me angry!" or "I'm sorry. I promise it won't happen again."

. . . AND WHY IT ISN'T HELPFUL AT ALL:

Getting blamed by a parent for his or her out-of-control behavior makes the situation twice as scary. You're not only fearful, but you're being told you're at fault for causing the situation. And the person who is actually causing the situation may feel entitled to punish you the next time you accidentally set them off. Getting an apology and reassurance isn't helpful because it's not going to stop the pain. Even if your parents believe they're telling the truth, you have seen that things don't get better and do get worse. The lack of a realistic, achievable plan on the part of someone who's supposed to be in charge to make things better gives you no hope for things getting better.

WHAT YOU THINK YOU NEED TO FIGURE OUT IN ORDER TO FIX IT:

If you're worried about the threat to someone else in the family, you want to figure out how to draw the fire to yourself instead. And if you're worried about a threat to you, you want to figure out how to duck and avoid attention. Whatever you're worried about, you just wish there were a way to make everyone stop and realize how destructive their behavior is.

WHY THOSE FIXES WILL FAIL:

Whether you lie low or take the brunt of a parent's anger, preventing an episode from getting worse or stopping the next one may be impossible. And your attempts to do this may exacerbate their frustration and guilt, which could make the next outburst even worse. Even if it were possible to gain the strength to get an out-of-control parent to back down, taking on the responsibility for everyone's safety and security would leave you with little freedom to lead your own life. Even worse, it could put you at risk of becoming out of control yourself.

WHAT YOU CAN ACTUALLY DO ABOUT IT:

Don't try to do the impossible. Don't make yourself totally responsible for protecting your family or punishing those who are creating the problem. That's far beyond your power and won't, in the end, help anyone. Instead, ask yourself whether there's something you can do that will make a positive difference for you and your family. If you think someone in the family is really going to get hurt, tell a teacher, a counselor, or a doctor. Aside from deciding whether to ring the alarm bell, your goal is to find things to do that will make you stronger and keep you out of the line of fire. One is to pursue activities and interests away from your home, from getting a part-time job to studying/hiding out at the library. As you already know, you can't stop a parent from losing control, and the more responsibility you put on yourself for their behavior, the less they put on themselves, which just makes things worse. However, the more independence you gain for yourself, the better able you will be to tell them that you love them and want to spend more time with them—while telling yourself that it's only if they can gain control over their behavior, which is their problem, not yours.

RED FLAGS TO LOOK FOR IN THE FUTURE:

Even if you find yourself repeatedly exposed to the same scary situations and awful feelings, don't let them take over your life. Your job is to find and maintain friendships and do things that can help you grow and distract you from troubles that are inescapable, but not your fault. Do not stew about family conflicts that are way beyond your control. Although you may feel helpless and responsible, that person in this scenario is the parent who is trapped in a bad behavior pattern and can't do better. So don't give up on yourself or your future or become fixated on ways to vent your anger or drown your pain. Instead, find ways to protect your sense of purpose and rise above the situation.

THE UN-SUGARCOATED SUCKINESS YOU CAN EXPECT:

There's no way to control the negative feelings or the sense of responsibility that living with fear and conflict causes, particularly if a parent lays a guilt trip on you for causing their problems or not doing enough to help. These feelings may push you to pick fights, give up on yourself, sacrifice yourself to protect others, or behave like either a bad person, a person who has stopped caring for themselves, or both.

THE UNTRUE SUCKINESS YOU MUST REJECT:

Surviving a scary situation isn't just about making it out in one piece, but making it out with your values, hopes, and sense of self intact. Being a survivor of an abusive situation does not mean you'll turn into someone who is bitter, vengeful, or forever damaged. Yes, there will be lots of painful feelings you will have to swallow without knowing when or how you will be able to let those feelings out, and you may not be able to stop anxious thoughts and nightmares for a long time to come. But if you can tolerate those feelings and pursue the same important goals all good and reasonable people share—growing up, becoming independent, and treating others well—you will eventually emerge strong from this extreme trial. You are not doomed to become an abuser yourself. If anything, surviving this experience will give you the unique insight to help create a world where people are valued and need never fear abuse.

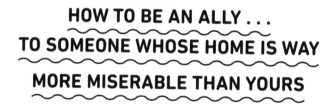

HOW TO BE AN ALLY . . . TO SOMEONE WHOSE HOME IS WAY MORE MISERABLE THAN YOURS

THE PROBLEM:

One of your close friends is always finding excuses to stay at your house. Even though he won't admit it, you know it's because his dad is always on his case and he hates going home.

WHAT YOU WANT TO DO:

Assure your friend that his father isn't acting like a

parent. And even though it's totally unrealistic, you wish you could get a big tough guy to go to his house and tell his dad to back off.

. . . AND WHY YOU SHOULDN'T:

Any attack on his father, even if it's just criticism meant as support, will make your friend feel disloyal, defend his dad, and blame himself. Then he'll feel uncomfortable around you and lose both his friend and his safe space.

WHAT YOU CAN DO:

Without directly dissing your friend's father, ask your friend to honestly ask himself whether he really deserves his father's criticism. Either way, let him know that you respect his ability to tolerate it and find ways around it. And tell him that he should tell you if there's anything else you can do to make living with it easier.

HOMES SUCK . . .
When Everybody Thinks
Your Home Is Weird

EVERY FAMILY CAN BE A little embarrassing once in a while. Some families, however, seem to always attract the wrong kind of attention. Even if you all get along well at home, the way people unfairly judge your home can make it hard for you to get along with everyone outside it. However, you can learn to ignore what people think about your family and prevent others' ignorance from interfering with your growth and confidence. If you can do that, then no amount of judgment will embarrass you. If anything, you'll feel embarrassed for those who judge.

HERE'S AN EXAMPLE:

My dad had a stroke a couple of years ago, and he hasn't been able to talk very clearly or move one side of his face since then. Otherwise, he's a totally normal guy, but he does look and talk kind of weird until you get used to it. I don't like to warn people about it when I invite them over because I think they should treat him like they would anyone else, but I guess most "new friends" can't do that because after they meet him they aren't eager to come back. After I heard that some jerk was spreading a rumor that my dad's "retarded," I gave up on everyone. I don't want to be ashamed of my family but I don't want to be friendless, either.

SIGNS YOU MAY BE MISINTERPRETING THINGS:

As always, it's possible that you're just being oversensitive and overly self-conscious about your unconventional family situation. Even if you have heard a few nasty remarks from one or two kids, that doesn't really represent what most people think.

. . . AND SIGNS YOU AREN'T:

You've been brought up to be proud of your family and have never hidden that part of your life from anyone. Or maybe you've never had a reason to feel self-conscious about your family until recently. So being overly sensitive about what strangers think isn't the issue. You trust your friends, tend to be positive, and take most things in stride, so you're not too sensitive about them, either. And the occasional nasty remark from one or two bullies has never prevented you from finding friends in the past, before everyone decided to consider your family weird.

WHAT YOUR PARENTS SAY TO TRY TO HELP:

"If you like yourself, what people think about your family won't make any difference," or "If kids are mean and judgmental about your family, then they're not worth paying attention to."

. . . AND WHY IT ISN'T HELPFUL AT ALL:

You've never met anyone who was so confident that he didn't care what people said about his family. So the idea that you shouldn't care seems unrealistic. Not only that, the assumption that you should be able to not care implies that your unhappiness is a kind of weakness, which it isn't. Some of the people who think your family is weird are usually pretty decent, so you can't convince yourself that they think that way because they're just prejudiced jerks.

WHAT YOU THINK YOU NEED TO FIGURE OUT IN ORDER TO FIX IT:

You would love to find a way to make your family seem

normal, or at least get everyone to see that the stuff about them that's different isn't really that important. You're not proud of this, but sometimes you wish you could pretend to be from a normal family.

WHY THOSE FIXES WILL FAIL:

You know that you can't change your family or the way the entire world thinks of them. They are who they are. And trying to educate the world about your family's uniqueness doesn't seem like the best use of your time. Hiding your family will just create more problems. And you're not sure what you'd need to do to become amazing enough to make people ignore your family, but you're pretty sure you have neither the time nor the genie to make that happen.

WHAT YOU CAN ACTUALLY DO ABOUT IT:

You're an individual with your own choices to make, not just a member of your family unit. And you define your own strength and achievement not through how you defend or redeem your family, which is seldom worth the effort, but through how you cope with your family's hard times or reputation as being weird. So don't try to change your family, the way people see them, or the feelings you get from being looked down on. Instead, make the best of family relationships by treasuring the love, care, and good times with them. Get what you can from school and any other hobbies, activities, or extracurriculars, and focus on old/real friends who know better. Then, if you can stay focused on doing your work and being a decent person, despite the negative attention that comes from your family name, you have done yourself, and your family, proud.

RED FLAGS TO LOOK FOR IN THE FUTURE:

Beware of letting the feelings of being unfairly judged give you a chip on your shoulder or lead you to pick fights. Don't let what other people think of your family define how you act in general.

THE UN-SUGARCOATED SUCKINESS YOU CAN EXPECT:

You're probably going to have to deal with judgmental jerks for a while, which means that new friends may be hard to find. It will always feel unfair to be criticized or punished because of the way people feel about your family. But like your unusual, lovable family, that's just another unchangeable thing you must learn to accept.

THE UNTRUE SUCKINESS YOU MUST REJECT:

Just because some people dismiss or misjudge you

because of your family doesn't mean you should think less of yourself. Don't try to punish the unfairness with more unfairness. Being a decent person when the world has treated you and your family unfairly is an amazing achievement. Don't let the jerks who care about you the least rob you of your values, which are the things that you should care about the most.

HOMES SUCK: THE POINT

Although your family is supposed to protect you and help you grow, there isn't much you can do when the family you're stuck with does the opposite. Your uncomfortable home life is due to bad luck, not to anything you've done. So don't think that you or your family are failures if you find that the situation under your roof makes you miserable. What will determine your future is not how well you can stop that pain but how determined you are to find a good path for yourself in spite of it. Looking back, you may judge your family in the same way; not by how unhappy it was, but by how much it helped you grow in spite of all the hurt it may have caused. You may not be able to do much to improve your home life, but you can improve yourself and your plans for the home you will one day make for yourself.

CHAPTER SIX

SEXUALITY SUCKS

IT'S COMMON TO WANT RELATIONSHIPS, even from a really young age. As you get older, the reasons for having relationships multiply, the feelings in those relationships become more intense, and the nature of the relationships becomes more complicated. Eventually, you may find yourself wanting a relationship that is more exclusive, committed, and possibly sexual.

While relationships are challenging, living without them, or just trying to figure out how to get one and whom you'd even want one with, is just as hard. Romantic feelings can cause a great deal of confusion because they can make you forget about less pressing, yet more important goals while trying to navigate them.

That's why, when looking for relationships, you have to be careful not to lose sight of your other priorities. Your main focus shouldn't be on finding love and "fixing" yourself in order to do it. Your true goal, as always, is to find what you think it means to be a good person and to do your best to live up to that, regardless of whether it impresses and attracts anyone else.

Romantic rejection feels especially personal. But ironically, because the reasoning behind who and how we love is the least rational—love and lust aren't exactly based in logic—it's actually the least personal rejection of all. It's not unusual to have trouble figuring out whom you're into or why the person you like isn't into you. Yet it's important to understand that, fundamentally, the source of the trouble isn't you. Especially if you're staying true to yourself.

HOW TO FIGURE OUT FOR YOURSELF WHEN SEXUALITY AND RELATIONSHIPS SUCK:

At some point, you might start to think about the kind of person you want to be with. But so many of the things you're expected to consider—nerd or jock, shy or outgoing—are of the least importance. You can't figure out whether someone is good for you until you determine what you think it means to have good character, for yourself and for someone you're interested in. Don't lose sight of those values, even if you get caught up in all the emotional stuff that relationships can bring. Here's a quiz to help you figure out whether you and the person you're into have the important character qualities that really count.

1 **You tell your girlfriend that you love her, and she responds that she likes you but her feelings aren't as strong as yours and might never be. You respond by:**
A) Saying you were joking because you actually totally agree with her and she should forget you said anything in the first place. Then you make an excuse to leave so you can go cry for two solid days and figure out all the things about you that will doom you to a lifetime as an unlovable loser.
B) Resorting to any tactic possible, from begging to blackmail to bullying, to get her to admit that she feels the same as you do. Either way, she has to love you as much as you love her.
C) Telling her that you're disappointed and sad and that you'll need time to get over it. But you hope to be cool enough with it one day to be friends again.

2 When you say something to your boyfriend that you meant as a joke, he overreacts, takes what you said as an insult, and gets in your face in a way that seems totally inappropriate and maybe a little bit scary. You react by:

A) Immediately apologizing for being so insensitive and cruel. You also make a mental note to never try to joke with him and only praise or agree with him.

B) Getting back in his face and making it clear that *nobody* disrespects you that way. You tell him that if he even tries to speak to you like that again, he'll regret it.

C) Taking a step back and apologizing for unintentionally hurting his feelings. You also make it clear that nothing you could ever say, even if it was intentionally insulting, would justify his reacting with that much anger. You won't tolerate being spoken to in that way, so if he can't learn to manage his temper better, your relationship won't have much of a future. You then give him space until he's willing to apologize.

3 The girl you like is nice to you over text or when no one else is watching. But she's kind of mean or just ignores you if you're around her when she's with her friends. You decide to:

A) Go with it, because you're happy just to get any positive attention from her, even if she hides it from everyone and pays no attention to you when there's an audience.

B) Force her to make up her mind, because it's either you or her friends. And if she chooses to stay with her friends, then she's just made herself a new enemy.

C) Let her know, the next time you see her one-on-one, that you're not comfortable with how she's treating you. If she's ashamed of how she feels about you then that's something she has to figure out. And until she treats you with respect, you respectfully decline the terms of this relationship.

4 **You find yourself becoming really into this guy whom you actually kind of hate. You disagree about everything and bicker all the time. Everybody assumes you only fight to hide the fact that you like each other. But even if you are into each other, the bickering is real and doesn't seem to be stopping any time soon. So you think that:**

A) Whatever creates this spark between the two of you is a good thing and worth the price of being perpetually irritated.

B) Yes, it's weird, but you've never walked away from a fight before and aren't going to start now. So you'll stick with it, as long as you get the last word.

C) You should try to have a real conversation with him about whether the thing between you is based on anything real. Because it seems that, after a while, romantic tension just becomes regular tension, and that's not such a healthy thing to have in your life.

ANSWER KEY

IF YOUR ANSWERS WERE MAINLY As:

Your values are too selfless. You're so focused on other

people's feelings and needs that you're ignoring your own. It's good to be sensitive to what other people feel in order to avoid conflict. And sometimes you can't help caring about and admiring someone more than you do yourself. But there's such a thing as caring about someone too much, especially if those feelings blind you to their flaws. You have an obligation to protect yourself, pay attention to your own priorities, and make your own judgments.

IF YOUR ANSWERS WERE MAINLY Bs:

Your values are too selfish. You're far too fixated on your own needs. It feels good not to be vulnerable, particularly if you've been dumped or hurt in the past. But always having to win or have the last word will turn you into someone you don't want to be. It also won't build the kind of give-and-take that makes a relationship healthy and rewarding in the long run. Believe it or not, greater strength comes from being confident in your ability to treat people decently than from knowing you can get them to do what you want or that you can never be hurt.

IF YOUR ANSWERS WERE MAINLY Cs:

Your values are well balanced. You've developed a smart way to protect your own needs while being sensitive to the needs of someone you care about. It will always require thought and often leads to second-guessing. You'll have to determine whether you're doing right by yourself and/or being too easy or too harsh on someone you care about. It's hard to do, but making hard choices always is. What you can feel good about is that you're doing your best to be a good person.

DO MY PARENTS HAVE A POINT?

WHEN YOUR PARENTS SAY . . .

"I don't know what's wrong with the girls at school that they don't like you—I think you're a real catch!"

IT SOUNDS DUMB BECAUSE . . .

They're obviously biased. And weird, because they're your parents and talking like this is gross.

BUT IT'S NOT DUMB TO THEM BECAUSE . . .

They genuinely love you, think you're great, and don't understand why other people don't see what they see, too. In other words, yes, they are biased, but at least they're honest.

SO BE SMART AND . . .

Appreciate that they're saying this out of love. If you're really feeling lonely and sorry for yourself, take this as an opportunity to remember that, no matter what the nasty voices in your head say, you are loved, valued, and seen by at least one person as worth being with (even if that person is responsible for half of your DNA). It may not be convincing now, but if your parents are saying you have the qualities to be a "real catch" when you're older, they might know what they're talking about.

THEN RESPOND BY . . .

Asking them to imagine for a second that they didn't create you, raise you, or even know you, and then tell you what they think is really great about you. Because you honestly don't see it sometimes, and you'd like to be able to tell yourself that you won't feel this way forever. Also, you'll get a nice reminder that you have worthwhile traits, and maybe your parents won't be so quick to respond so grossly in the future.

SECTION 1

SEXUALITY SUCKS...
When You're Unsure About Gender or Sexual Identity

NAVIGATING THE WORLD OF SEX and relationships is hard enough as it is. But if you find yourself attracted to unexpected people or identifying as an unexpected gender, it can add a whole new level of confusion and chaos. It can be hard not to believe that there's something wrong with you that needs to be hidden, changed, or grown out of. You may not be able to change whom or how you love or what other people think of it, but you can learn to control your fear of

sexual differences if you take your time and remember to focus on being a good person, period.

HERE'S AN EXAMPLE:

I've always had crushes on girls since I knew what a crush was. But now I'm kind of freaked out because I think I'm into this guy I just met through my cousin and I don't know what's happening. I don't think he's gay, but I've never really thought about this stuff. Now I don't know whether I'm gay or I'm whatever, because there are so many labels out there and up until now, I didn't spend much time worrying about it. I just want to know what's happening and who I really am.

SIGNS YOU MAY BE MISINTERPRETING THINGS:

Sexual traits, which are the features you have, and urges, which are what you feel attracted to, are two very different things. You may find that you aren't comfortable with the sexual traits you have, or that you have sexual urges for someone with the same sexual traits as you. Obviously, this can all be fairly confusing, especially when you're encountering sexual urges for the first time, as there's no way to know how strong they're going to be in the future or whether they're going to change over time. So you have reason to be unsure about your sexual identity, because it takes time to be sure, and questioning your traits and urges is what gets you thinking in the first place.

. . . AND SIGNS YOU AREN'T:

Unlike the guy in our example, your urges and traits, or lack of them, haven't changed in a relatively long time. And you've wanted them to change so you can avoid your sexual preference or gender being different from most of your classmates.

WHAT YOUR PARENTS SAY TO TRY TO HELP:

"Kids your age get lots of wild ideas and experiment, but you'll get it out of your system," or "If you don't like this part of yourself, then that's your heart telling you that it isn't really you."

. . . AND WHY IT ISN'T HELPFUL AT ALL:

The problem with being assured that these thoughts will go away is that the thoughts may not go away. And if they're here to stay then it's really hard to accept your new normal without feeling like you're failing in some way. That's when reassurance isn't reassuring and makes you feel more unusual and abnormal than ever. Not liking a part of yourself doesn't mean it's broken and that you need to fix it. It's our differences that make us unique and human. So expecting that you should be able to get rid of everything about yourself that you don't like just makes you feel like a double failure, because you're not only imperfect but unable to improve.

WHAT YOU THINK YOU NEED TO FIGURE OUT IN ORDER TO FIX IT:

You'd like a method for wrangling all your thoughts, traits, and urges back into line with whatever's normal, acceptable, and free of frustration. You'd also like a definitive test that would tell you exactly what your true gender and sexuality are so there'd be no confusion for you.

WHY THOSE FIXES WILL FAIL:

There's no way to get all your sexual traits and urges, or your thoughts in general, under total control. And your traits and urges can change as you mature, and maturity can sometimes be a long process. Besides, definitive proof of gender or sexuality wouldn't necessarily result in acceptance. It usually takes people time to get used to change, especially if it's unexpected or unconventional.

WHAT YOU CAN ACTUALLY DO ABOUT IT:

In a fair and just world, we'd be encouraging you to live your truth ASAP, because you'd be able to honestly discuss your experiences with and concerns about sexual traits and urges and always be accepted and understood. In this world, however, such discussions are not always easy. Your friends and family may not want to hear what you are trying to tell them, particularly if you choose to share information at a bad time, in a misguided way, or with a good person who has the wrong prejudices. So put as much thought and research into your communication as possible and don't accidentally narrow your options or encourage people to categorize you in a way that turns out to be inaccurate by committing to a label or identity when you don't have to. Guard your privacy until you have a chance to share and reveal what you choose. If possible, find an adult or adviser with whom you can talk about your situation and who can help you decide when and under what circumstances you want to be honest with others. And if there isn't a trusted adult around, carefully select a peer group online where you can find people going through the same discovery process as you, as they will be open and accepting.

RED FLAGS TO LOOK FOR IN THE FUTURE:

Avoid possible conflict about your sexual or gender identity by dodging the topic with people who may not be entirely accepting. Fights with others about your sexual identity can be exhausting, impossible to win, and dangerous to lose. Even if they're in the wrong, you can't control their prejudices. And trying to do so will distract you from those more realistic everyday goals that are far more important in the long run.

You should also be careful not to rush your discovery process by throwing yourself into risky situations, like by getting too involved with people you barely know! The reddest of flags is when your feelings of rejection and alienation push you to start doing everything you can to reject your core values and rules. It will turn you into someone you are not and drive away people who could be able to help you.

Bottom line: Don't let being mistreated by jerks push you to forget yourself and what's really important and become a jerk yourself.

THE UN-SUGARCOATED SUCKINESS YOU CAN EXPECT:

You may not be able to avoid feeling worried about how your sexual feelings and traits will affect your future. And you may not be able to stop yearning for acceptance from people you love and respect while knowing you won't get it. The inability to manage sexual yearnings and frustrations may also affect you, proving painful and dissatisfying.

THE UNTRUE SUCKINESS YOU MUST REJECT:

As hard as it is to deal with frustration, fear, or conflict, don't blame yourself for having negative feelings or evoking the nastiness of jerks. You know how little choice you have over sexual feelings and gender identity. But even if you did have a choice, you also know that we can always choose how we treat other people and what our values are. The responsibility for how you're being treated belongs to the people being unkind, not to you. Finally, sexual identity doesn't define you. It's just one of the many elements that are part of your makeup. Determining your values and how to live up to them is most important. Whom you ultimately love or what gender you live as is always second to how you treat others and yourself.

HOW TO BE AN ALLY . . .
. . . TO THOSE DEALING WITH SEX-
AND RELATIONSHIP-RELATED ISSUES

THE PROBLEM:

Friend A confides in you that she has a massive crush on friend B. You happen to know it isn't mutual.

WHAT YOU WANT TO DO:

You want to tell her straight up that B is not into her and this is going to end in tears.

. . . AND WHY YOU SHOULDN'T:

You may be helping your friend avoid heartbreak in the long run by being frank. But she may not believe you, she may blame you for her heartbreak, or she may accuse you of being jealous. She may then insist on hearing it from the source, who may also blame you for embarrassing them.

WHAT YOU CAN DO:

Keeping friend B out of it, tell friend A to just face the music and tell friend B, tactfully and positively, that she wants to be more than friends. Ask friend A to be prepared for rejection, not because you don't believe in her, but because friend B already sees her as a friend and might not be able to see her as anything else. And tell her that no matter what friend B says, you have her back.

Sex You Can Watch
Isn't Sex You Should Have

If you're lost in a strange neighborhood, can't remember the capital of Texas, or just yearn to see a rat eating a whole slice of pizza, having a phone or tablet available to save the day is a truly great thing. On the other hand, there's a whole bunch of stuff online that isn't so useful, funny, or even true. One thing that's sometimes hard for parents to talk about—with their kids or just in general—is the easy availability of videos and images of adults having sex.

Sex is always awkward to talk about, and every parent has their own way of talking about it with their kids. But what makes talking about these images and videos especially difficult is that they don't truly represent what sex between two people who love each other really looks like. In other words, the sex you may see online can't actually teach you much about what to expect or want from sex in real life.

That's because, in real life, people have sex to express positive feelings about each other, whether it's true love or a moment of passion. In real life, sex is supposed to feel good for both people involved, but the sex you see online is just supposed to look good, even if it may actually feel uncomfortable, humiliating, or even painful for one or both people involved.

And of course, the sex you see online is preplanned, so nobody is seen taking the crucial real-life step of getting consent before doing anything to or with their partner to make sure they're both interested. In real life, you're the one who determines when you're ready to have sex and, with your partner's consent, what you want that sex to be like. And nobody has the right to pressure you or assume you want to do things you're not comfortable with, no matter what they've seen people do online.

There's nothing wrong with being curious about sex, and educating yourself about sex is a smart, responsible thing to do. But if your source of information about sex, be it a video online, a suggestive pop song, or an especially braggy friend, focuses more on exciting you than presenting you with factual information, then that's not a source you should trust.

Ultimately, as the actress Jameela Jamil put it, trying to learn about how actual, real-life sex works from those online videos and images is like trying to learn how to drive from watching *The Fast and the Furious*. All you're really learning is how to crash and burn.

SECTION 2

SEXUALITY SUCKS . . .
When You Feel Like a Lonely Loser

AT THE ROOT OF LOSERDOM is the feeling that you're undesirable and alone. And while being ignored or rejected by others is painful, it usually happens for reasons beyond anyone's control. If there's no one around whom you want to date or who wants to date you, it's seldom because you're doing anything wrong. In any case, as long as you keep working hard to learn, grow, and be a decent person, you can't lose anything (except your ability to care about what jerks think). More importantly, you can learn how to stay positive, even while waiting for life to take you to a time and place where you will be able to meet people who like and respect you for you, and develop special relationships that are worthwhile.

HERE'S AN EXAMPLE:

I've never been able to get girls to like me, and I can't imagine how I ever will. My parents keep telling me that it's cool to be a nerd now, but wherever they're getting that, they're wrong. It's not just that girls don't like me, but the kind of guys that girls like don't like me. I have a group of guy friends who are as nerdy as I am, and there are girls at school who are just as geeky and nerdy as us. But most of the time I just feel really alone. I know that feeling so bummed and lonely just makes it worse, because the guys I hang out with complain that I'm too much of a downer sometimes. But I can't help it. I just imagine myself doomed to a life without dates, sex, or love, and it feels hopeless.

SIGNS YOU MAY BE MISINTERPRETING THINGS:

Just about everyone gets a little freaked out when they first attempt to talk to someone they're interested in, so it's possible that you're just nervous. And you may have convinced yourself, perhaps in order to protect yourself from being hurt, that they'll never be interested in you and it's not worth even trying. It's also possible that you intimidate anyone who might be interested in you. Especially if you're always with a group of friends. And as always, you may find it hard to meet others because you struggle with being oversensitive, anxious, or down on yourself.

. . . AND SIGNS YOU AREN'T:

Even when you've found the courage to approach someone, their lack of interest has often been unmistakable. So you know you're not just wimping out or getting in your own way by being too nervous or intimidating.

WHAT YOUR PARENTS SAY TO TRY TO HELP:

"There's someone for everyone, just you wait," or "It will be easier for you to get dates if you're friendlier, have a better attitude, and stop being so down on yourself!"

. . . AND WHY IT ISN'T HELPFUL AT ALL:

You've done your best to be friendly, approachable, and optimistic. And still no one seems to be interested in you. You've thought about changing your look, but you know you wouldn't want to be with anyone who didn't appreciate your style.

WHAT YOU THINK YOU NEED TO FIGURE OUT IN ORDER TO FIX IT:

You'd like to know exactly what to say and wear, how to act, and how to be the kind of person that other people find attractive and are interested in being around. That way you could both find someone to be with and lose the fear that overcomes you whenever you even think of talking to someone you like.

WHY THOSE FIXES WILL FAIL:

Unfortunately, outside of classic movies about high school (many of which are older than your parents are), you don't know of anyone who has found the secret to mastering social interaction by borrowing someone else's image. That's something you have to find out in your own way, in your own time. We all need to find a strategy and language that work just for us, and that's something even adults struggle with.

WHAT YOU CAN ACTUALLY DO ABOUT IT:

Since we've established at this point that there's no magic word, simple exercise routine, or free app that will give you the confidence and/or skills to effortlessly get and show interest, it's more important to focus on what you can't and shouldn't do about being on your own. It's hard to feel good when no one seems to want to talk to you or you're feeling vulnerable, shy, and sensitive. So don't give yourself a hard time for it, or for being too sensitive to make the first move, or for being afraid of rejection. While nothing feels more personal than rejection, the truth is that the things that feel most personal in life usually aren't. For example, if you're bullied, it's usually because a mean person has randomly decided to make you their latest target, not because you've done something to deserve the torment. And if you're invisible to or rejected by someone you're attracted to, it's often not because of you specifically. They may just be into someone else, or they may not be worth your time, anyway. In the end, your social success depends to a huge degree on luck, which is something you don't control and for which you're not responsible. So don't let your bad luck at that moment turn into discouragement or self-blame. Rejection and loneliness are always going to hurt, but knowing that you haven't caused your pain and don't deserve it should make them easier to bear. And don't let those feelings stop you from getting your work done and being involved in activities. Pursuing your own interests, regardless of romantic status, will make you more comfortable with others, help you build confidence, and maybe even attract someone worth your time.

RED FLAGS TO LOOK FOR IN THE FUTURE:

Don't allow your disappointment to push you to become isolated or prone to lashing out. Don't let the pain of your situation make you feel that you need to put people down or punish them for what you're going through. And don't let solitude stop you from focusing on your schoolwork and interests.

THE UN-SUGARCOATED SUCKINESS YOU CAN EXPECT:

There may be times when you can't stop feeling rejected, inferior, or self-conscious. You may not be able to avoid comparing yourself to people who seem to have a much easier time establishing relationships. It may be hard to fight thoughts in your head about what's wrong with you that make you feel lonely and unwanted when others don't seem to have that problem.

THE UNTRUE SUCKINESS YOU MUST REJECT:

Being alone doesn't mean you have to feel lonely. Often, it's the things we do with our lives, not the people we do them with, that make life fulfilling. So work hard to reject the feelings of loneliness and self-pity by continuing to do the things that mean something to you. Stay focused on school and pursuing your own interests, regardless of who does those things with you or appreciates your dedication.

Remember: You Have to Be Okay with Being Alone

At the end of the day, the only person you're guaranteed to be with in this life is *you*. Friends and family are important, but if you're not willing and able to be alone and keep your own company, even when loneliness makes it hard, then you'll become desperate to find someone, anyone, to be with. And that will include people who are mean, unreasonable, and likely to make you way more miserable than being by yourself ever would.

Rejection can make loneliness especially unbearable. Ironically, though, the thing that can make you feel like the most isolated, lonely person on earth is an experience shared by almost everybody. As sad and lonely as rejection may make you feel, you've now joined the universal club of the rejected. Take comfort in that, and instead of letting the pain push you to make bad choices, use the experience to become more comfortable being alone and less likely to be as stung by rejection in the future.

Some people may wonder how you can be with someone else if you don't love yourself, but the love they're referring to isn't the kind you have for a crush, partner, or Glamazonian superstar. It's the love you have for close friends, because even though they get on your nerves or do things you don't like, you still care about them deeply and will always have their backs. Being your own best friend doesn't mean you always love yourself, but you will always stand up for yourself and protect yourself from toxic people who don't like, respect, or treat you as well as you deserve to be treated. Then, even when no other friends are around, you're never really alone.

SECTION 3

SEXUALITY SUCKS . . .
When You Can't Get Any

IT'S TOUGH TO RESIST A strong physical
urge, like having to hold in a sneeze during
a music recital. And sexual desire, of
course, can often fall into this category.
It's often made worse when it seems like
everyone but you is having sex. But when
you're younger, the pleasure that comes
from having sex is often outweighed
by the frustration, confusion, and
heartbreak that can come after. The
desire to have sex makes you much
more vulnerable to heartbreak and can
also push you to use people whom you
would otherwise treat with respect. To

manage your urges and outside pressure, you must refuse to think that frustration equals failure. Remember the solid goals you had for yourself, like being a good person, before this nagging, distracting desire kicked in. Those goals are the hardest to reach, which is how you know that they're the most important and the truest measure of your success.

HERE'S AN EXAMPLE:

I'm the one person among my friends who has never had sex, and it isn't because I want to be a virgin. I have friends who are girls, and I'm not afraid of talking to girls in general, but they like to treat me like one of their own. They've made it clear that they could never see me as anything but a pal, which makes me feel like the biggest loser around. And I'm sure that makes me even less appealing to them as a guy. I don't know how to turn it around and get a girl to date me, or just let me see her topless.

SIGNS YOU MAY BE MISINTERPRETING THINGS:

It's possible that people find you attractive, but there may be reasons they can't or won't act on it, like being intimidated by you or unsure if you see them as "more than a friend" yourself. And even more possible is the chance that most of your friends who claim to be sexually active are not. You may be overly sensitive to your lack of experience, to the point that your friends would be less likely to tease you if you weren't so touchy. Or you may just be too focused on sex, so it's creating issues when there don't need to be any.

. . . AND SIGNS YOU AREN'T:

Your friends are usually honest, so you feel fairly certain that they're not lying about their experiences. You've been careful not to get touchy when people tease you about "not getting any." And you don't think you're more fixated on sex than anyone else you know. It's just that everyone else seems to want or get something different than you do.

WHAT YOUR PARENTS SAY TO TRY TO HELP:

"If only you could just work harder and focus more on school than dating," or "Who you give your virginity to is the most important decision you'll ever make, so give it time to see if what you and she feel is really love," or "Think more about having a good friendship, and romance will follow."

. . . AND WHY IT ISN'T HELPFUL AT ALL:

We humans have little control over our urges, whether

that's for sex, food, or another episode of whatever we're bingeing on Netflix. So the idea that you could make a sexual urge disappear by just trying harder or being a better person is both wrong and insulting. And even though some classmates or your parents might say the opposite, losing your virginity isn't necessarily that important in the long run. What is definitely important when you decide to have sex with someone is that your judgment isn't so clouded with emotions that you put your heart and your health at risk. Even when you're sure you won't let it happen and that you're trusting the right person, sex can make you very vulnerable to heartbreak, just as pushing sex too hard on others can make you act like a jerk. And yes, friendship will help a romantic relationship last, but it can also confuse things when you're into someone you're friends with and she just doesn't see you *that* way.

WHAT YOU THINK YOU NEED TO FIGURE OUT IN ORDER TO FIX IT:

You sometimes wish you could just find someone to have sex with and get it over with. Or you'd like everyone to agree to stop caring about sex so much, or at least care about it less, so that having it, or not having it, wouldn't be such a big deal.

WHY THOSE FIXES WILL FAIL:

Losing your virginity will likely create more problems than the one it's intended to solve. Being in a rush means you may choose someone you barely know or trust. And that could set you up to be taken advantage of or to take advantage of someone else, and generally throw your values and self-worth out the window. You'd be making sacrifices that just aren't worth it. When getting physical comes before actually getting to know and like each other, the risk of rejection is higher and the resulting rejection can be even more painful.

WHAT YOU CAN ACTUALLY DO ABOUT IT:

If you're not careful, the overwhelming pressure to have sex can create serious risks, not just for doing something foolish, but for distorting your idea of intimacy in general. At that point, you need to take a step back and do some serious thinking. There will always be factors you can't control. But the more thought you give the situation, the more confidence you will have in your ability to protect yourself and act decently, regardless of the pressure you're under to have sex. So get as much information about sex as you can. That information should include not just figuring out your own feelings, but also information from trusted professionals about the basics of sex and how to protect yourself and others, physically and emotionally, when you're feeling sexually ready. The more you know, the easier it is to have a realistic idea of sex, not just in terms of the act, but in terms of the circumstances and consequences. And when you ultimately figure out all that, you'll realize there's often no clear path to finding or creating intimacy at this point in your life. You just have to start thinking of the bigger picture, do what you think is right, and be prepared when the right person comes along.

RED FLAGS TO LOOK FOR IN THE FUTURE:

It's difficult when you're so preoccupied with having sex that it distracts you from your real priorities. That can lead to you compromising your values, morals, and self-worth. You're in real danger if you can't see yourself as successful or respect yourself unless you find a way to have sex. That could give you the justification to do possibly inappropriate or risky things that would make you respect yourself even less and could seriously hurt someone, including you.

THE UN-SUGARCOATED SUCKINESS YOU CAN EXPECT:

There's no escaping how strong sexual urges, and the stigma of virginity, can blind you to the consequences and risks that intimacy involves. You may feel envious, humiliated, and frustrated about your situation. And it may be very hard to have those feelings and still get through every day.

THE UNTRUE SUCKINESS YOU MUST REJECT:

When you can't get something that you really, really want, whether it's sex or straight As on your report card, it's natural to feel you lack something basic. But that feeling is misleading. You have very little control over the obstacles life puts in the way of finding someone who not only wants to be with you, but is actually worth being with. And despite what all those outside and inside forces tell you, sex does not and should not define or validate your existence. If you can't keep things in perspective then you're putting yourself at risk, not just for possibly doing very stupid things in order to have sex, but for developing a distorted and unhealthy idea of intimacy in general. Basically, many of the commonly held ideas about virginity—that you're ugly, a loser, or a freak if you're still a virgin past a certain age so you must get rid of it as soon as you can—is a total load of BS. If you think hard about what makes sense for you, you'll feel confident that you're doing right by yourself and see how wrong so many of your peers' ideas about virginity and sex really are.

A Quick Guide to Consent

Your average health/sex ed class covers the biological basics, giving you the fundamental information you need to make safe, smart choices. Unfortunately, those classes rarely cover the topic of consent. And understanding consent is as crucial to your sexual education as anything on a diagram of the human body.

Basically, consent means *permission*. You need consent in order to be intimate with someone, because, simply put, you should only be intimate with someone if you want to be with them *and* they want to be with you.

It seems straightforward, but all too often, signals can get crossed. One partner can make assumptions, push the other, or ignore signs, often without meaning to. Or a partner can feel too insecure or unsure of themselves to make it clear that they're uncomfortable and not consenting to what's going on. And if consent isn't clear and respected—if both people involved aren't in total, clear agreement about what's happening—then you risk being hurt, hurting someone, or even committing or being the victim of a crime.

The simplest way to make sure you have consent when you're intimate with someone, of course, is to ask if what you're doing or what you want to do is okay. It may be awkward, but you can't assume that the other person is always on the same page as you, especially when you're just getting to know each other in this new way. You also have the right to say no or stop what's happening—to withdraw your consent—at any time, and have your wishes respected.

That means that, if you ask for consent and the other person says they're not okay with what you're suggesting or doing, then *you have to stop what you're doing*, period. Don't stop for a bit and then try again, or try to talk the other person into it. As hard as it may be, you have to let it go.

In reality, anatomical diagrams are the only simple things about sex. It's much harder to teach or understand the heavy emotions, urges, and personal connections that are also involved. It also takes a while to figure out what you're comfortable with as you become sexually active.

That's why it's important to know that, while you're

learning and figuring things out, you and your partner should both have a say in what you do together. Because intimacy may be technical *and* emotional, but if you understand what consent is, it's more likely to also be enjoyable and fun.

SEX SUCKS: THE POINT

The overwhelming pressure to have sex and figure out who you are as a sexual being can make it really difficult to see sex for what it is. It's basically a bodily function that pushes you into a close relationship with another person. It also creates strong urges that make it much, much harder for you to select someone who is truly appropriate for you to be close with. Sex should be performed safely with both parties' mutual consent and understanding and with minimal risk to your body, mind, and future. That's why it's so important to try to ignore the noise that comes from the media, your friends, and anyone else and judge for yourself what's important about sex and sexuality and the personal circumstances that would make having sex the right choice for you. Much of what's most important about sex—like your traits and urges, and its availability—you don't control. Time will make you comfortable with whatever gender traits and urges turn out to be yours. As long as you don't let the absence of romantic relationships become an obsession or shape the way you see yourself and others, you'll be the one deciding when and how to let intimacy into your life, rather than letting those things be decided for you.

ACKNOWLEDGMENTS

MICHAEL I. BENNETT, MD, and SARAH BENNETT:

Thank you to our editor, Sarah Fabiny, who masterfully ninja'd apart a massive manuscript into something worthwhile. Thanks also to our agent, Anthony Mattero, who made our dreams of writing a book for younger people (while still keeping a bad word in the title) possible. A last-minute thanks to Sara LaFleur, our diligent proofreader. Thanks to the Stein, Nadelson, and Cotton families, with whom Sarah grew up, and alongside whom Michael and his wife raised their children. We appreciate having you in our lives and watching your families grow. Thanks to our daughter/sister Dr. Rebecca Anderson—a surgeon who, unlike her shrink parents, actually cures patients—and to her husband Aaron and their brood. Special thanks to awesome dad/drummer/fellow-author Jeffrey Salane (jeffreysalane.com), who first suggested the idea of this book. Finally, all thanks to Dr. Mona Bennett, mother/wife/master of our universe.

MICHAEL I. BENNETT, MD:

I would like to thank the following: My father, Jacob Bennett, whose bedtime stories were about heroes who didn't always win battles or save the day, but who did the right thing when life was unbelievably hard. He was my hero. My teachers at Upper Canada College, who taught me the value of embracing pain for the sake of values. My Saturday-school teacher Heinz Warshauer, who survived the Holocaust and led a program that taught caring and tolerance. Rabbi Emil Fackenheim, who taught the same kids that being good was the only thing that deserved real respect (though happiness would be nice). Uncles Arthur and Max Robinson, combat veterans, who protected me from the violence that gave them their PTSD. Buddies Bill Johnston, Jim Arthur, George Biggar, and Brian Watson, who helped me survive the pain of school, as valuable as it may have been. My sister and brother-in-law, Naomi Bennett and Peter Bleiberg, who helped talk these ideas into the dream of a book. Daughter Sarah, who honors me by asking me to write with her. And my mother, Beatrice Bennett, who was brilliant, caring, and devoted. If she'd been any easier to manage or understand, I never would have been motivated to become a shrink or write a book like this.

SARAH BENNETT:

To my teachers Mr. Zilliax, Mr. Hardy, Mme. Schram, Mr. Gilpin, Ms. Atkins, Ms. Smith, and all the others who, like Mr. DeLetis, made learning bearable (and even occasionally fun?). I hope you are all retired and enjoying a rum drink on a hammock somewhere far from frozen New England, with no young people in sight. And apologies to any great teachers I might have forgotten, as I've been fairly successful at repressing most of my memories from before I turned twenty-five.

To all the friends I have thanked in my previous books (a statement I am also thankful and flabbergasted I get to make): Angela Boatwright, Paisley Strellis, Lizzy

Castruccio Kim (and the extended Castruccio and Kim *familias*), Molly Templeton and Steve Shodin, Tobias Carroll, Alex Eben Meyer, Ali Chenitz, Quinn Heraty, Ashrita Reddy, Diana Rupp, Tabitha Lee, Andi Vettros, Candi Kreinbrink, Amy Baker, Liz Gallagher, Kesone Phimmasone, Mary Lordes, and Zach Broussard. Thanks to family (or almost family) Eyan and Mary-Jane Mitchell, Eilene and Bill Russell, and Sherry and Richard Lee.

As always, thanks to Cristie Ellis, Rebecca Onion, Elanor Starmer, and Julia Turner. Together, we have survived high school and our twenties and thirties, and are now surviving the adult slurry of careers and parenthood and everything else. Thanks to Emma Forrest and Maysan Haydar, who got to skip the high school part but have been with me through almost everything since.

Finally, this book is really for the next generation, i.e., the many offspring of the people listed above. Hopefully, this book will help make your school years far less sucky than mine were.

FURTHER RESOURCES

Compiled by Ann Goebel-Fabbri, PhD

WEBSITES—THESE OFFER EDUCATIONAL INFORMATION AND REFERRAL RESOURCES, AMONG OTHER THINGS:

Anxiety and Depression Association of America. "Find Help for Eating Disorders." https://adaa.org/ find-help-for/women/eating-disorders.

Multi-Service Eating Disorders Association. https://www. medainc.org.

National Association of Anorexia Nervosa and Associated Disorders. https://anad.org.

National Eating Disorders Association. https://www. nationaleatingdisorders.org.

Recovery Record. https://www.recoveryrecord.com.

Recovery Record is a tool to bridge what happens in therapy and what happens in your daily life. It is not intended to take the place of therapy. In fact, there is a clinician and patient version, so that your treaters can use it to augment what you are doing together in therapy.

BOOKS FOR PARENTS:

Siegel, Michele, Judith Brisman, and Margot Weinshel. *Surviving an Eating Disorder: Strategies for Family and Friends*. 3rd ed. New York: Collins Living, 2009.

Teachman, Bethany A., Marlene B. Schwartz, Bonnie S. Gordic, and Brenda S. Coyle. *Helping Your Child Overcome an Eating Disorder: What You Can Do at Home*. Oakland, CA: New Harbinger Publications, 2003.

BOOKS FOR TEENS:

Cash, Thomas F. *The Body Image Workbook: An Eight-Step Program for Learning to Like Your Looks*. 2nd ed. Oakland, CA: New Harbinger Publications, 2008.

Fairburn, Christopher G. *Overcoming Binge Eating: The Proven Program to Learn Why You Binge and How*